When you Became
My Life

When you Became
My Life

Anshul Sharma

Srishti
PUBLISHERS & DISTRIBUTORS

Srishti Publishers & Distributors
N-16, C. R. Park
New Delhi 110 019
editorial@srishtipublishers.com

First published by
Srishti Publishers & Distributors in 2013

Typeset by Eshu Graphic

ACKNOWLEDGMENTS

Thank you, God!

I am deeply indebted to all my colleagues and teachers. I never ever thought during my college days that I will miss all those faces to this extent some day in life. I love you all. Please be with me forever. All my dreams and views for this life are a gift from all of you. Many thanks for being a part of my life. Writing about all of you would mean another book in itself; so kindly adjust. You all know very well how lazy I am!

I would like to express my gratefulness to Mr Brij Khandelwal, Mrs Ritu Lavania, Miss Amore Singh and Srishti Publishers for their valuable suggestions and constant support.

PREFACE

I have attempted to write something that makes me different; neither good, nor bad, but different from others. But, dear readers, please forgive me, as I am not perfect. All I wish to earn out of this is a small place in your heart. And for that, I will try my best.

I'd like to share a couplet that inspired me:

Ghar ki tameer chahe jaisi bhi ho, usme
Rone ki kuchh jagah zarur rakhna...

It can be roughly translated as: no matter how wealthy your abode may be, keep some space spare for crying. Absolutely true! To weep is an integral part of life. If you want to laugh whole heartedly, then you must understand the value of tears; if you want to experience something sweet, then you must remember bitterness; if your heart is revelling in the joy of victory, then you must not forget that setbacks have their own value.

So, even if you dislike me, it is a surety that I'll get your love. Everything revolves around love; I want your love. Because praise, admiration, applaud and other things are short-lived. But love remains in the heart; it exists forever. From this page onward will begin my journey into your heart, to make a place for itself inside it.

Part-1

1

SUICIDE

The belief that death finishes everything, closes all matters and ends all woes is wrong. How can we forget that the soul exists even after death! God and soul are immortal. Why forget that there is no substitute for purity of love? There are times when loneliness haunts us; we want to cry. Pain screams somewhere deep inside us. Despite having many people to share things with, we still feel lonely; we share our feelings within ourselves then.

Agra, 01 September 2011

10:00 a.m.

I was standing inside a Shani Dev temple situated on the banks of the Yamuna River. Praying to him about the one thing most graduates wished for – an appropriate, well-paying job." I was busy discussing my demands and wishes with god when something happened. An old man appeared before me out of nowhere, and advised me to work hard for good returns: "*Beta, mehnat karo; phal zarur milega*".

I was so petrified, my first reaction was to scream a loud "f**k!". Somehow, what came out of my mouth was a sober, "Yes, uncle".

I closed my eyes tight enough to not be able to see him. Wanting to be sure that the old man had moved away, I opened my eyes slightly. I felt relaxed seeing him walking towards the river. In his presence, my conversation with god about my problems wouldn't have been possible.

I am an engineer by degree, and unemployed by profession. I know very well that I have not valued my studies, but at least I was able to complete it.

After trying to convince God for about fifteen more minutes, I looked around to see if the old man was trying to eavesdrop. But he wasn't there; he stood on the bank of Yamuna. I turned my gaze back to Shani Dev. Suddenly, a splashing sound startled me. I noticed ripples and bubbles on the water surface. Someone must have jumped into the river! The incident happened so suddenly that I couldn't react. I knew it was common for people to take bath in the river, but I couldn't take my eyes off the place where that man stood. I could make out it was not anything routine. The man had not surfaced yet; he had no control over the rough waters of the mighty river. I was sure it was a suicide attempt.

I froze for a moment, didn't know what to do. It suddenly dawned on me how foolish it was of me to have bunked swimming lessons; it was costing someone his life.

I went blank for a moment with no idea what to do. From where I stood in the courtyard of the temple, I could see a man drowning in the water, while on the other side shopkeepers were selling their goods. In such a threatening situation, there was no option but to shout for help.

Men came running from all corners, seemingly impatient to know what had happened there. I pointed towards the boy and they ran to save him. I followed them.

It was amazing to see that all of them were experts. They formed a human chain by holding each other's hands and pulled the boy out of the water. He was in his mid-twenties, and from his clothes seemed to belong to a respectable family. He was panting, his heart beating fast. He seemed quite anxious. I was shocked and wanted to know why he took such a desperate step.

The boy was mumbling something; I bent down to hear it. "Fuck off," he said. First as a murmur, then as a shriek. He was shouting at the people who had just saved his life.

That angered me and I asked him, "What's wrong with you, dude? You should be thankful to these people. They have saved your life…"

He ignored me and started moving towards the road. His behaviour was peculiar. He was clearly upset with life.

I was curious to know what could have led such a young, respectable person to hate his life in such a way. So I ignored his anger and went ahead to ask, "Hey, dude! I know it's your life but you can't be so thankless to people who put their own lives in danger for a stranger. Why did you think of taking such a drastic step? You can share with me; I promise I won't judge you."

He mumbles some inanities again and I feared the anger in his eyes, so decided to walk away.

As I turned around to leave, I heard a panic-stricken voice, "Hey, buddy! I am sorry."

I turned to look at the defeated man standing with folded hands. "I am sorry," he said again.

"No, no. I am sorry. It's your private life and you were disturbed already. I shouldn't have instigated you. I am sorry."

"It is not your fault at all. My life is so scattered that I was compelled to take such a decision. Now for me there is no aim in my life for which I should remain alive. My life is empty."

He had tears in his eyes, glistening over his wet cheeks. I knew he was upset and tried to help him, "If you feel comfortable, then you can share your problems with me. I am sure you will feel better."

He smiled for a moment, reassuring me for a brief time. "Yeah, you seem like a nice person. The way I behaved with you was unpardonable, and you still wanted to help me out. I don't know why but you seem to be the right person with whom I can share."

Despite his easing out, I couldn't dare to ask him, directly - why did you attempt suicide? I invited him to sit with me on the riverbank with an added request, "And only if you promise me that you won't jump into the water from there."

He chuckled and assured me that he won't try this again.

He started talking now, "Can I know the name of the person who is taking so much interest in me?"

"Of course, my friend! Ever since I was born, my mom and dad have called me Sam."

"That's a funky name."

"So Sam, what do you do?"

"I am an unemployed engineer, searching for a job. I have completed my engineering a few months back. But why all these questions about me? You tell me. What do you do, other than this attempt of suicide?"

He chuckled at my statement before saying, "My name is Neev Singh. I am from Dadri, Haryana."

That surprised me. Had this chap come so far for this? I managed to blurt, "From Haryana? Didn't you find a place for suicide in Haryana?"

He laughed, and I noticed his ringing laughter. "You are right, Sam. I don't jump into rivers so frequently. It's a long story."

"I love stories," I said. "Would you mind sharing it with me?"

"Why would I stop you if I minded? And you cannot change my fate for me."

I smiled, "Neev! Why do you want me to change things for you? I just wish to know what happened."

"Sam, I just wanted to say that my story is not very interesting. It will not be very fascinating to hear."

I wanted to explain that it was not about interest or disinterest and I did, "The fact is that I want to know what made you upset enough to take such a step."

He looked at me in the eye, and his eyes had so much pain hidden behind them. He started in a philosophic tone, "Sometime we cannot define life; it looks like a zigzag pattern, confusing and chaotic. And then we think, what is the purpose of life? What do we want? Some say the purpose of life is to ensure that one does not come back to this planet, because it is bereft of love and even when there is love, it is painful." He paused and chuckled, "We have been educated to operate a computer; nobody teaches us how to live life fully. Most of us fail when faced with the force that makes up for our life. . . ."

2

COLLEGE

Dadri, Haryana, July 2008

It was the happiest day of my life; I graduated in commerce. I shared my happiness within my own little world – my students. They come to me for tuitions, and are like an alternate family for me. My happiness knew no bounds because this was the first step that would take to the big plans I had for my future.

Though cancer rendered me motherless when I was ten, I knew she would have been very proud of me today.

I was thinking back on the days when my father started running his general store. He remained isolated, as he had no one to share his feelings with. Our financial condition was not sound; the shop was the only source of income and was not sufficient to survive.

Like it is said, misfortune never comes alone. After my mother's demise, my father could not handle the pressure and became addicted to alcohol. I continued to suffer. My school fees could not be paid timely. I wept bitterly, because I remembered my mother. That's when I started teaching small children, to be able to pay for my education.

When the clouds of misfortune started clearing, and I began relaxing, God worked his whip again. My father came to know that I have started earning; he gave up all else and became reluctant with his work in the shop. One day, he told me to sell the shop, for he found it useless to sit there without any profits. I could gather that he didn't like to sit in the shop. He looked unwell too. The doctor confirmed my fears; alcohol had damaged one of his kidneys. Replacing a kidney would cost around two lakhs, an amount I could not have been able to gather without selling off the shop.

The shop was sold off for a lakh and the money was put into my bank account for use in future.

April 2009

I was taking tuitions along with my studies at college. After a few months, I had managed to save a good twenty-five thousand rupees from my teaching. And for my father's treatment, I needed to arrange about another lakh.

In many ways, I convinced my father to not drink. But he had become a habitual drinker by then. He didn't care about his life and, of course, about me. He always wanted to have another way for arranging money for drinking.

One day during my class, a peon came to me and said, "Sir, there's a phone call for you from the hospital".

It did not take me long to gather who it could be about. Without wasting a minute, I left for the hospital on my motorcycle.

I drove fast enough to cover the ten-minute distance in about half the time and entered the doctor's cabin without any permission.

"What happened, sir?" I asked, panting. "Is everything okay?"

"Neev, I have a bad news for you. Your father's other kidney has also been affected due to alcohol and we need to transplant a kidney as soon as possible otherwise we won't be able to save his life."

This had been inevitable, given his drinking. I asked the doctor how much it would cost to transplant a kidney. I knew the figure would be way beyond my reach, but I wanted to know. The doctor repeated mechanically what he had told me the last time, "It would take two lakh rupees for each kidney and fifty thousand rupees for transplanting it".

I had managed to save around 1.25 lakhs, but that was not enough. Still, I told the doctor to save my father and I would somehow arrange all the money.

The doctor agreed and asked me to relax, telling me repeatedly that everything would be fine.

Both of us left the cabin and moved towards my father's room.

I saw him from outside the glass wall. He was in deep sleep, resting. I was equally restless, with tears rolling down my cheeks. I was scared and did not know how I was going to arrange the money.

The first thing I did was to arrange those 1.25 lakh rupees from the bank and deposit them to the hospital, so that the process could begin. After depositing the amount, I rummaged names of people in my mind who could help me with the funds in this situation. I could take a loan from someone and return it later. I tried to contact many of the lecturers in college, but to no avail.

I needed money, and quickly. The only option I could see left for me was to sell the house. And I did that. I never once thought where I would go and live if the house is sold or where my father would come back to. At that time, it was a choice between my father and a house.

We had a small house, but I was sure to get around five lakh rupees for it. The property dealer lived next door, and knew well that I needed the money urgently. He told me that he could give me only three lakh fifty thousand rupees, not a single rupee more. I felt beaten by life and I had to accept his offer.

I agreed and signed the statement and took all the money in cash. After depositing the money in the hospital, I had to wait for an hour. I had deposited four and a half lakh rupees and I had to pay the remaining twenty-five thousand. All I wanted was my father's recovery.

I felt helpless; my subconscious bringing back memories of my mother's death. It made me shiver; I don't want that again. Every minute was spent as a lifetime. The fear of losing him was immense and it weighed on my heart. —On an impulse, I folded my hands and started praying to god for my father's well-being. Tears were rolling down my cheeks as I knelt down to pray.

I was looking at the operation theatre again and again, just to get any news of my father. A ward boy came out of the room. I asked him, "What happened? How's my father?"

He didn't answer, scaring me even more.

I was too insecure to think what was happening inside. Without knocking, I entered the operation theatre and saw my father lying on the bed, unattended. The doctor stood in one corner, punching something into instruments blinking LEDs.

I was confused; the doctor should be with him. It seemed I had lost my voice, but I managed to ask the doctor, "Is my father safe?"

He came near me, trying to console me and said the two harshest words of my life, "Sorry son. We could not save him. The new kidney which we had transplanted was also infected due to spoiled liver. I am sorry."

My eyes were brimming with tears, my heart was beating fast, and words refused to come out. I just sat on the floor, wondering who I was now going to live for. My world seemed to have collapsed right in front of my eyes, and I could not do anything to save it.

The times I had spent with my father came back to haunt me. Even the vision was blurring out and I knew that they'd leave just faint memories behind.

I was losing my will to live with each passing moment. I was just twenty years old, and the worst phase of my life had begun.

I performed the last rites according to the Hindu religion with the remaining twenty-five thousand rupees. After everything was done, I was left with a meagre 2500 rupees left to begin a new life.

The place made me remember my parents, I had no house to call my own, the shop had been sold, and out of all the friends I had in college, I was in touch with one – Aadi. He was working in his hometown Agra as an accountant when this tragedy hit me. Though he Could not come and meet me, we were in regular touch. After my father's death, he had been continuously forcing me to move to Agra for good and leave behind all sad memories. He had even promised me a job in a college as a lecturer and a room on rent. He advised that I change the place to be able to forget the pain. I was touched with his words of concern; I also realised he was one of the very few people who had not changed with my times. Aadi had always been my closest friend; he understood me as much as my parents did. We shared everything with each other and after a long time, I was eager to meet him...

I agreed to his proposal and decided to start a new life in a new place. Agra, the city of love, the city of the Taj Mahal.

Aadi was happy to know my decision and offered to pick me up from the Agra bus terminal after my three-hour-long journey because it was my first trip to the city.

As I sat by the window seat, all giddy and nauseated with the smells inside the rickety bus, I realized how difficult it is for a person to leave his birth place. And then it struck me, I no longer have a home here, nor anyone to call family.

Since I did not have a mobile phone, I was worried for Aadi because he would be waiting for me at the bus stand. The bus conductor shouted out to me, telling me that Agra was the next destination and a couple of minutes away.

The mention of the new city made me nervous. This was the first time I was supposed to stay alone. But Aadi would be here; my lone trustworthy contact in a new city.

The moment alighted from the bus, I saw Aadi standing in front of the tea stall, sipping tea from a small glass. His eyes met mine for a split second and he roared, "*O Haryanvi chora agaya re*".

He asked the *chaiwala* to make another cup – *malai maar ke* – and rushed towards me to hug me. I was visibly touched by his affection, and whispered a "thank you" as I hugged him.

"Shut up, Neev! There is no place for thank you between friends . . . and we are best of friends. I have arranged for everything; you should feel at home here.

He asked about my father, gave me his condolences and tried to bring me out of my sadness. In a fit to talk about something else, I asked him where he had taken a room for me.

"Oh that! It's the room right next to mine in my house," he was beaming.

"Shut up, Aadi. I am not going to give you any more trouble. Please make arrangements for me at some other place."

"Hey, don't you worry. We had given that room out on rent earlier on as well, and the paying guest has left the room only about a couple of days back. If you feel uncomfortable staying with me, then take that room on rent and give me whatever you feel is right."

I smiled, because I knew he won't let me stay anywhere else. I was also left wondering if he had thrown his paying guest out on purpose.

He also told me that he had fixed up an interview for me in the college he was working in the very next day. I felt relaxed after knowing that I would be joining in the same college where Aadi was working. After finishing the '*malai*' tea, we moved towards Aadi's house.

When we reached Aadi's house, his mother was standing at the gate, eyes on the road, and his father was reading the newspaper. Aadi led me in and warm smiles greeted me. I removed my shoes and entered, touched uncle, aunty's feet. Their eyes reflected sympathy for me; this was a familiar look on people's faces for me these days. Aadi cut the moment short by introducing me to his parents. He told me that his father was retired from BSNL and mother was a housewife. I was trying to smile at both of them, but anyone could have made out that it was fake.

Aadi had a big home; two floors were made with a partition. One side of the floor was meant for the family and the other for the paying guest. I was surprised that the three of them had such a huge house to themselves. Knowing that I had just lost my little house back home very recently, he just patted my shoulder and smiled.

He then started showing me around the house. He stood outside one of the rooms and said, "This is Aashi's room. My younger sister. She is pursuing graduation first year with commerce and you are going to teach her in college and at home. She is a bit weak in Accounts and I remember, you have terrific command over it."

I was grateful, but did not want to insult his friendship by saying thank you again and again. I knew in my heart he was God-sent. I only managed to joke, "Oh, now I have understood that all this help is not for your friend. You needed a PG and a tutor, and what better than a smart guy like me."

He quickly defended, "No, no, no! It's not like that, Neev. Trust me!"

I chuckled, "Oh, Aadi. I was just joking. I know you too well to mean that." He was visibly relieved to hear that. I added with warmth, "Thanks for everything, yaar. It will be my pleasure if I can do something for you."

"Forget all that has happened, Neev, and start life afresh. Lay the neev, the foundation, for a new life from today. Okay? And it's 7 p.m., you should go freshen up. I will call you for dinner in a while. Maa's making something special, thanks to you."

I hesitated, "Aadi, can you do me a favour? I would like to have dinner at my room itself. I don't want to interrupt your family in any way. I will feel a bit odd to have food with all of you. I want to stay here as a paying guest, not as a friend. I hope you'll understand and not feel bad about my saying it."

"Neev, we would not have any problem having you sit with us. You're family, too. But if you want to be alone for a while, it's okay. I will ask Aashi to bring your food in your room."

Aadi left the room and I was again alone. I was still missing my dad. I was unable to forget him, as I had spent lot of time with him.

I began unpacking to divert my mind. While hanging my clothes in the cupboard, I found a photo of my dad in my belongings. Remembering the past days, my eyes filled with tears. I sat on the floor and froze in the corner thinking of my father. I felt lonely. The thought that I had nobody to call family, who would take care of me made me numb. While sitting in the corner, I heard a sound of footsteps on the stairs. I controlled my tears. Then someone pushed the door open and I saw a girl standing right in front of my eyes. She wore a red-coloured *salwar kameez* which suited her fair complexion and deep eyes very well. She was an epitome of beauty and had flawless skin. She seemed like an angel: the glow on her face reflected her innocence and lovable nature. She was looking for me, her eyes roving around the room. I was sitting in the corner, behind the bed. So even though she could not see me, I could see her big bright eyes.

Then she noticed me.

"Sorry, sir. Have I disturbed you? I should have knocked the door," She sounded apologetic and scared.

"No, it's okay. I am fine. You are…?"

As my confused eyes were seeking an answer, her big eyes smiled as she told me her name: "Aashi Sharma".

"Oh yes, I know you. Aadi had told me about you, Aashi."

She eased a bit, "Sir, I have brought dinner for you. But I think you are not feeling comfortable here. Should I call Aadi bhaiya? Why are you sitting on the floor?"

"No, Aashi. I am fine. Please don't say anything to Aadi. I have already disturbed all of you. I got a little upset; hopefully with time, everything will be fine. Why are you still holding the plate? Please put it on the table."

"No, sir. It's not like that. You should take care of yourself. And please have your dinner on time."

"Yeah, definitely. Thanks, Aashi."

And she left the room. With the way she was talking, I was sure she knew everything about me.

I took a shower and moved towards the table to have dinner. But as soon as I put the first morsel into my mouth, my mood suddenly changed. I did not feel like eating.

I looked around the room and surveyed what else I had in the room. It was mostly bare with a few pieces of furniture - table, chair, a bed and a window which opened into the opposite phase of the house. From the window, I could easily see the complete house. One window from the opposite side opened exactly in front of my window. I guessed it'd be Aadi's room. I was peeping to see what he was up to when I caught a glimpse of Aashi doing some work in the room. I closed my window, hoping she had not seen me staring into her room.

I came and sat on the bed, thinking about my interview the next day. Suddenly, somebody knocked on the door. I thought it'd be Aadi, but when I opened the door, Aadi stood there with Aashi, uncle and aunty.

I let them all in and aunty asked me with great affection, "*Beta khana kha liya?*"

I felt guilty saying, "Not yet, *aunty ji.*"

And excitedly Aashi shouted, "See! What I told you was correct.'

Aadi hushed her, "Will you be keep quiet for a while, Aashi? Please."

I gathered that Aashi must have told them that I had been crying and that's why they all had come to see me.

This time aunty spoke with greater affection, "Beta, you should eat your food on time, otherwise you will start feeling weak."

I could only nod in agreement.

Aashi threw another squeaky sentence at her mother, "Who will eat if you cook *aloo gobhi?*"

Aunty's face dropped and even though I did not like the dish myself, I said, "*Aloo gobhi* is one of my favourites. Really."

Aunty cheered up instantly, and everyone smiled.

Uncle came forward and putting a hand on my shoulder, said, "Don't ever feel you are alone, beta. We are like your family. If you need anything, just let us know."

My eyes filled with tears, and I choked on my own words, "Thank you so much for everything".

Aadi came forward and hugged me. He said, "Neev, tomorrow will be a new day for you. The interview is at 9:00 a.m. The college is five minutes away; we'll walk together. Okay?"

"Yes, I will be ready before you are," I joked.

Aashi blurted again, "Enough family drama! Let him sleep now".

Everyone wished me good night and they headed out of the room. As I stood to close the door, I heard Aadi complaining to aunty, "Mummy, Aashi talks too much".

And they all disappeared.

I locked my room from inside and started eating the food. While I was having food, I don't know what exactly happened to me. I was thinking of Aashi's joke on "*aloo gobhi*" and started laughing. I finished my food and got ready to sleep. Searching for the light switch, I landed right next to the window.

I was just about to press the switch when I heard a faint knock on my door. Wondering who it could be, I moved back to open the door.

It was Aashi.

"Sorry to disturb you, but Mummy had forgotten to give you the blanket. You will need this at night."

"Oh! That is so sweet of you, Aashi. Thanks a lot.

Aashi smiled and went into her room and i locked the door behind her, hoping that it'll be opened the next morning now.

I spread the blanket on the bed and moved to the window to switch the lights off. Coincidentally, Aashi was standing beside the window and doing something I couldn't fathom. I switched the light off and hit the bed.

I began thinking of my father; how much I was missing him. Teary eyed, I dozed off.

My morning dream broke with the sound of *arti* coming from somewhere close. My wrist watch flashed 6:00 a.m. It was ridiculously early in the day for anything, leave aside singing *artis*. I woke up from my bed and moved towards the window. I was surprised to see the whole family and some other people standing together and worshipping.

It took them an hour to complete their ritual. And all the while, I couldn't sleep.

I was sleepy, but got ready for the interview by 8:00. I was hungry, and was waiting for the breakfast. But it looked distant. Moreover, I was shy enough to ask for it, too.

Suddenly, I heard Aadi's voice, "Hey Neev, come on! Let's move to college."

I picked my bag full of documents required for the interview and moved downstairs. Aadi was standing with his bag, ready to go.

"Good morning, Aadi."

"Good Morning, Neev. Hope you slept peacefully."

"Yeah, it was good. And the *aloo gobhi* was really good."

Aadi and I chuckled.

Aadi shouted again, "Aashi we are getting late."

Aashi shouted from the stairs, "I will be there in seconds."

We three marched towards college. After getting out from the gate, Aadi asked me, "Hey Neev, did you take your breakfast?"

I turned towards Aadi and saw Aashi's eyes going wide. She shouted, "Oh sorry, sorry. I am really very sorry. Mom had given me the breakfast, but I forgot to offer him."

"What! Aashi, are you crazy? How can you forget to give him breakfast? He has not eaten anything because you forgot! Now how will he manage till afternoon?" Aadi was visibly angry.

Aashi looked sad and sorry, so I tried to rescue her, "Hey, Aadi. It's okay, I am fine. I don't take breakfast anyway; I have a habit of taking lunch and dinner only."

"No dear, you will feel hungry. College will be over by 2:00 p.m. I will ensure that we have some food in the college itself and Aashi, you make sure to 'not forget' things from tomorrow. Okay?" Aadi chided.

Aashi flushed and apologised yet again.

We reached college soon after. It was a big college, having four separate buildings. By the looks of it, it seemed like a good college. Lost in such thoughts, my eyes went to the board on top of the gate, "Gyanlal Girls College".

I asked perplexed, "Aadi, is this a girls' college?"

"Oh, I am sorry. I forgot to tell you. Is there any problem with this being a girls' college, Neev?"

"No, no. It's fine. I was just asking." We were hesitating to speak openly because of Aashi.

She moved towards her classroom and Aadi took me to the Dean's office. He asked the peon to let the Dean know that I had come.

I was nervous, but when I looked towards Aadi, he smiled and said, "Don't worry, it's just a formality."

The peon come out of the Dean's office and asked us to go in. Aadi walked ahead of me and gave me a sign to follow him. He opened the door and said, "May we come in, sir?"

I saw an old man in his mid fifties sitting behind a huge neatly arranged wooden table. He shouted, "Hey, come on in Aadi! I was waiting for you."

Aadi interrupted and said, "Sir, he is my friend. Neev Singh."

I said, "Hello, sir".

"Hello Mr. Neev. How are you?"

"I am fine, sir."

"Well, your friend has told me about your experiences. I must say these are hard times, but you should be strong and have faith in god. He will make everything fine."

"Yes, sir," I simply nodded.

I handed over my resume to him and he began reading through. He looked quite impressed with the profile and he even said, "Well done, dear".

"Thank you, sir," I felt a hint of a smile escape from my lips.

The Deam smiles in response, "So, Neev, as per your experience, you have a good command in Accounts. I hope you do a great job here also. You can go and meet Miss Aliya Singh in the staff room. I've told her about you and she will let you know about all your duties."

"I will do that right away, sir. And thanks a lot."

"Don't mention it, Neev. You deserve it. And one more thing, I will discuss your salary with our accounts manager, who is your friend. He will let you know. Hope that is okay with you."

"Yes, sir. That'll be fine.

I came out of the office and asked the peon where the staff room was.

Since his mouth was full of tobacco, he pointed his right arm towards his left. I followed his gaze and saw a board that read "Staff Room".

I thanked him politely moved towards the staff room.

I knocked at the door and peeped in. The only lady, actually the beautiful lady who was sitting in the room, was around twenty years old and she had an impressive personality. The best part about her was the dress she was wearing. She saw me enter and got up from the chair, asking me, "Yes? How can I help you?"

"Actually I am looking for Miss Aliya Singh."

"You are talking to the right person, then," she smiled an enigmatic smile.

"Hello," I put my hand forward for a shake. I introduced myself and told her the Dean had asked me to get in touch with her. A glint of recognition assured me that she was aware of what I was talking about.

She looked around the staff room and said, "This is the place where you have to spend a lot of your time from today onwards."

I smiled and she continued, "This is the most amazing thing about lecturing: you like to teach and take only two or three lectures in a day. The rest of the time can be spent in the staff room."

She went back to the table and pulled out a sheet of paper from her file. It was my time table.

We were sitting on parallel chairs, very close to each other. I had no interest in the time table which she was discussing with me. I was thinking whether she was married or not. Though she was not wearing any *mangalsutra* or *sindoor,* I was still wondering. Then the thought that she must be having a boyfriend started bugging me. I was wishing she was single.

The only words that my brain registered were, "...got everything?"

I nodded nervously.

She must have seen the lost expression in my eyes, so she said, "You have the next lecture of Accounts in B.com 1st year, section A; and immediately after that in section B. You can sit here and relax the rest of the day.

I merely nodded. To which pat came a reply, "Please don't be uncomfortable with me. I am not your senior; I have only one year experience here."

"Oh, it's not like that, madam. It's my pleasure to meet you."

She frowned, "Hey, don't call me madam. It's just Aliya. And you are Neev."

"Okay Aliya."

"That's better. Let me introduce you to the section A, and then you can take your class."

The moment she got up and I realised it's time, nervousness hit me. It was my first time at teaching girls.

I put my book in the bag and got up from the chair. Aliya gave me an attendance register.

My body was shivering with anxiety, but I couldn't have looked back. This was my only chance of survival.

I remembered god and entered the classroom confidently. All the girls got up from their seats to wish us.

Aliya responded chirpily, "Good morning, girls."

One of the girls interrupted Aliya and said, "Ma'am, when will an accounts teacher be appointed? It's already been ten days.

"In fact, that's what I am here for. Meet Mr Neev Singh. He will teach you Accounts from today," she pointed at me, making all the girls in class stare at me simultaneously. I managed a faint smile, but my eyes were looking for Aashi. She was nowhere to be seen.

Aliya asked me to come over to the next section for introducing me. I followed her and the same introducing ritual happened in the other section also. The surprising thing was that Aashi was nowhere to be seen in Section B also.

Aliya took her leave, wishing me luck for the class in the A section.

I found myself standing facing forty girls. It was slightly embarrassing for me. It was a challenge for me, which I had accepted unwillingly.

In my nervousness, I greeted them, "Hello everyone. I will be teaching you accounts from today, and will put in my best efforts for it. But you will have to promise me that you will follow it seriously. I can accept everything but not carelessness in studies. Besides, I am here to help you and to solve your problems. You must never hesitate to share your problems with me. And I expect from all of you to maintain decorum (between a teacher and a student.)"

Everyone was looking at me, so I reassured myself, "Is everything clear and everyone clear on this?"

The girls shouted in unison, "Yes, sir".

I turned to the blackboard and started jotting down a few essentials for introduction to Accounts. When I turned around to face the girls, I saw a girl on the last bench. She was sleeping; her head was down. I asked the others who she was.

The girl sittign next to her woke her up. And I finally found who I was looking for – Aashi Sharma.

"Any problem?" I asked, trying to be strict.

"Yes, sir. A bit of pain in my head."

"Have you taken some medicine?"

"No, sir. I will be fine within a few minutes. It happens with me sometimes," she explained in a murmur.

"Okay. But if you don't feel comfortable, let me know."

"Okay, sir."

I continued with my teaching, but kept an eye on Aashi to ensure that her headache doesn't get worse, After some time, she had opened her note book. I could make out she was fine.

I finished my lecture and moved out from the class to take the other lecture in the adjoining section. When I finished with the lecture, I was getting out of the class when I saw Aadi standing at the gate.

"Hey, how was your first day?" He greeted me with a smile.

"It was fine, yaar. The credit goes to you," I responded.

"Don't say that. Let's go to the canteen and have something to eat; you must be hungry."

Aadi brought me some food and offered just one plate as he took his seat. I looked at him puzzled, "What about you?"

"No Neev, I am not hungry. I had breakfast in the morning. And sorry if you were disturbed with the morning *aarti*. This, I am afraid, you will have to adjust with, yaar."

I reassured him, "Hey, it's okay yaar. After all that you have done for me...

"Shut up, buddy. What are friends for!" He smiled and patted me on the shoulder. Then, as if remembering suddenly, he said, "And your salary is fixed. Just tell me, how much you got in Dadri?"

"It was around ten thousand rupees," I said with my mouth full of food. I was actually very hungry by then.

"And what are you expecting to get here?"

"The same amount. Why?"

Aadi looked shocked, "Neev, it's Agra. And you are teaching in one of the biggest college of Agra. Think big!"

He casually told me that the salary was fixed at double of that, twenty thousand per month, and after a year, when I begin teaching more classes, it'll be raised."

To say I was ecstatic would be an understatement, "Oh, my god! It was really unexpected. Thanks so much, Aadi."

"Don't thank me, yaar. You deserve every bit of it."

I was touched with the way he had been of help at almost every step, when I had come to believe that I had nobody in this world to call my own. I did not want to say thank you again, because he would have gotten angry. So, I changed the topic instead. "Hey Aadi, decide the rent of my room also."

He looked taken aback and feigned anger, "Shut up! We will decide it some other time."

"No, we will decide it right now; otherwise I am not going to live in your house." I was adamant; I didn't want to take advantage of his goodness.

"Neev, give whatever you feel fine. How can I fix the amount with you?"

"Okay, just tell me how much did your last paying guest pay to you?"

He sighed, "It was around three thousand rupees including food, light and water charges."

I smiled, "Okay, it's fixed. I will pay you the same amount when I receive the salary."

"Okay my dear, are you happy now?"

"Yup, now it's fine!" I ate in peace after that, and wished I could share this happy tiding with someone. I thought of my parents and how proud they would have been of me today.

I went back to the staff room and Aadi back to his duties. My eyes were searching for Aliya, because other than her, I didn't know anyone. And suddenly Aliya came in. The moment she spotted me, she shouted, "Hey dude, what did you do to the girls? They seem mighty impressed with you."

"Oh really? I hope they will cooperate with me in future as well." The day was going good.

"Don't worry everything will be fine," she assured me.

She came and sat next to me. An elderly teacher was sitting right across and watching us, but Aliya didn't seem to care. She started talking about her family, her studies, her classes, and within a few minutes told me everything I could have wished to know about her. But after finishing her entire introduction, she asked me to do the same too.

I was hesitant, but nevertheless told her about my past. After hearing of it all, she went quiet and a bit emotional, "Sorry Neev, I shouldn't have asked you all this".

It struck 2:00. Everyone started to pack up, but I didn't move from my place. I was overwhelmed by the sheer number of girls in the ground. I was wondering how I would find Aashi and Aadi. But, Aadi and Aashi both came to the staff room.

I asked Aashi, "How are you feeling now?"

"I am fine now."

Aadi interrupted, "What happened?"

I said, "Oh, nothing! She had a headache when I went to take class in the morning."

Aadi merely nodded. If we had the faintest of idea how much pain this headache was going to cause for us in the days to come!

We were home in five minutes. As we all headed back to our respective rooms, Aashi came to give me lunch in the room after a while and went back without any conversation.

I was a bit normal after spending a day in college because of favourable conditions there.

But still I had a lot of pain left behind by my father's loss. And for me, it was very difficult to share my pain with someone else because of my introvert nature.

I had started to adjust there, but couldn't share my grief with anyone. It'd be more appropriate to say that I didn't want to share my grief with anybody. My pain was mine; no one was allowed to enter my world. I was ok with my pain. Sometime I felt my grief was my only true companion which was remaining with me without any complaint and expectations.

Many phases come into our lives and go. Achievements and losses are part of life, but when grief becomes someone's true companion, this is really their misfortune.

3

DEATH RATE

Once again, music woke me up. "*Om jai jagdish hare...*" I practically began my mornings with complaints to god about this loud worship. I respect all this but at 6:00 am in the morning, it felt irritating. The *arti* went on for an hour and just when i thought I could sleep for another hour, someone knocked at the door.

I managed to open the door sleepily to see Aadi standing and smiling.

"Loser, first your father doesn't let me sleep with his singing, and now you," I joked.

Aadi started laughing, perhaps reminded of my naughty college-time image.

"Sorry yaar, but there was something important," he said casually.

I welcomed him into the room. He told me that he had an appointment with the doctor for his mom; he would not be going to college.

I asked politely, "What happened to aunty?"

"Nothing much; just severe back ache."

"Oh! Then you must see a doctor."

"That's what I told her. I have told Aashi to be in the corridor for you on time," he told me.

"That's not a problem; we will manage to go. Don't worry for Aashi," I assured him.

Aadi stood up, visibly relieved. He started moving towards the door, saying, "You can go back to sleep now, Kumbhakaran".

He chuckled and went out; I chuckled and hit the bed again.

When I woke up an hour later, I was sure of not getting breakfast, because aunty was not feeling well. Surprisingly, Aashi brought my breakfast. I thanked her politely, and she smiled.

9:00 a.m.

Aashi was waiting for me at the main gate. We started for college at the right time. I complimented her for the tasty breakfast she had prepared. Aashi smiled and said, "Bhaiya had made the breakfast today."

I was surprised. But since we did not have anything else to talk about, both of us were walking silently. Then suddenly, just about fifty metres away from college, a few boys started commenting, "Hey baby! Bunk college for today, have fun with us."

"Aashi, do you know them?" I asked her.

She replied in a worried tone, "Not at all. I don't know who they are."

There were four boys, two each on two bikes. While I was trying to figure out what was happening, one of them commented again, *"Kabhi humse bhi baat karlo. Talk to us also"*.

I was scared after seeing four of them. I did not know what to do. because I knew nobody in that new town. Still, I managed to say, "Hey buddies, don't tease the girl."

One of the boys commented in a harsh voice, "Wow, at last the hero is talking".

I was about to raise my hand on one of the hooligans when Aashi held my hand and asked me to leave from there quickly. She pulled me towards the college gate, saying, "These boys are not good; just ignore them."

It was really annoying and I was sure that Aashi was feeling bad.

Still she managed to regain composure and went ahead towards her classroom.

I was feeling bad about not having done anything over there. I kept thinking what Aashi would think of me that I couldn't do anything when four men were harassing her.

A few minutes after the incident, I was sitting in the staff room, thinking about it. For me, it was an unusual thing to have happened. I was lost in my thoughts when suddenly Aliya entered the room. She chirped, "Hey buddy, good morning."

I managed to smile and wished her back. Thereafter, she started discussing random, unusual things – about her new neighbour, the milkman, the vegetable vendor and what not. And then she spoke about her boyfriend who she was madly in love with! It broke my already pained heart further. She had discussed a lot with me from the very first day, apparently also because we were the only two people in the staff room who were not married, not too old and some fun to be with.

Nevertheless, there were some times when she bored me and I desperately waited for my lecture to start.

It was finally time for my first lecture, that too in Aashi's class. I was feeling nervous to face Aashi, but it was inevitable. She was sitting at her desk, and lowered her head slightly when she saw me.

I quickly looked at the rest of the class and wished the girls to announce my arrival, "Good morning, girls." All of them settled down, and I continued hesitatingly, avoiding eye contact with Aashi because she was doing the same thing.

I wrote "DEATH RATE" on the black board. I spoke at a higher volume to make Aashi attentive, "This is a very important topic and you will have numerical problems to solve on this, so please be very attentive."

I explained the topic to the students and then I saw a hand raised for a query. It was Aashi.

"Yes, Aashi. Tell me."

None of the girl was surprised that I knew her name, because some girls already knew that I lived as a paying guest in her house. Don't we also know about girls' network of passing information; it's far better than any other grapevine ever seen.

Aashi asked me in a heavy voice, "Sir, can you explain the entire topic in just one line? Just so that I can easily understand what exactly you are wishing to teach us."

For a moment, I was speechless. It's not possible to sum up an entire topic in one line, but I still tried. I also felt as if she was not clearing her doubt, but trying to insult me in front of the class. When I finished, she asked me again, "Could you explain all this in a simple language? I am waiting to know about this interesting phrase, 'death rate'."

I couldn't understand why she was asking such a thing or behaving like that. All my energy and confidence was going for a toss. But, thanks to Aliya, I could get out of the sticky situation. She knocked at the door and said in her lovely voice, "Time over".

Before moving out, I told Aashi, "You will get your answer in the next class."

It was convinced that Aashi was upset over what the boys did and what I did not do in the morning.

I went ahead for the next lecture and taught the same topic there also. But nobody pointed a thing out the way Aashi had. I had a perfect command over this topic, I was sure, but Aashi's cross-questioning made me feel that perhaps there was something amiss.

I kept myself busy with reading about the topic in the college library to be able to answer Aashi satisfactorily. When it was time to go back home, I prepared myself to face Aashi. Somewhere in my mind, I was scared regarding those boys, whom we had encountered in the morning.

I was standing at the gate of the staff room, waiting for Aashi to come. Moreover, I saw her from a long distance as she had perfect bold look, which made her recognisable to anyone from a distance as well. She came closer and I asked her, "Should we move?"

"Yes, of course, sir."

The air between us was thick with animosity, it seemed, with the difference that enemies fought in the battle ground, and we had fought in the classroom.

I was anxious lest we come across those goons again, but nothing of that sort happened. But throughout those five odd minutes, both of us did not say a single word.

We reached home, and Aadi opened up when Aashi knocked at the door.

"Hey, how was the day?"

"It was fine," I replied.

"And yours, Aashi?"

"Perfect," Aashi replied.

I was confused with her reply, but then we all moved towards our respective rooms.

I was freshening up, fully aware that within minutes, Aashi would be there with my food. However, surprisingly, Aadi came with the lunch.

"Thanks, Aadi. I was hungry."

Aadi smiled, "So finish it up fast."

He sat on the bed as I ate at the table. He was going through my books and suddenly said, "Hey do you remember Namita ma'am?"

"Of course, how can I forget her? You had an affair with her for a long time. By the way, is it still going on or is over?" I chuckled.

"Shut up, Neev. It was just a rumour; we were good friends only. Now she is a married woman."

"Oh!"

"Do you remember she used to live in a hostel?"

I looked up at him with a mischievous smile, "Yeah, I do. And I also remember that her room was attached to yours."

"Neev, don't remind me of those good times and memories," he looked lost in his own world.

"What memories are you talking about?" I asked after finishing my food.

He looked around and then got up from the bed to close the door of my room. I picked up my chair to have a seat closer to where he was sitting.

He started whispering, "Neev, it was the third semester for us and the first day for her. She was allotted the faculty room in our campus which was attached to my room. The other rooms of the students were in the other building. I was the only one living in that building; I can't say if it was pure luck or also the shortage of rooms in the hostel.

"I first saw her when she was shouting after having seen a rat in her room. It was around midnight and all other faculty members were sleeping but I was watching porn movies at my desktop. She knocked at the door and I was afraid thinking who could come at that time.

"I got up, upset at having been interrupted. I only knew that a new teacher had come to stay in the room next to mine.

"I opened the door and a beautiful woman was standing in front of me. I was pleasantly surprised and inevitably ended up thinking of the woman i was watching on my desktop. The teacher looked better than her. One look at her in the grey-coloured night suit and I fell in love with my teacher.

"However, it was with great difficulty that I managed to listen to her. Her face was red due to her fair complexion. She was shouting, 'There was a big rat in my room, please do something or call security. I am new to this place'."

"After hearing her, I couldn't stop myself from laughing, which obviously made her very angry. I asked her, 'Sorry, but how can I call security just for a rat?'

"She asked me, all hassled, 'Then who would sort this problem out? You?'

"I confidently told her I will and asked her where she had seen the rat. She indicated towards the table. I picked up a heavy stick to hit the rat. As I went closer to the table and tried to hit it, it ran out of the room. I looked at her and asked her, 'Anything else, ma'am?'

"She thanked me and asked me my name. After I told her the same, we bade good night to each other and went back into our respective rooms.

"I continued watching the porn movies more interestingly, this time assuming that ma'am instead of the actress. when the movie was over, I went to close the attached bathroom door in the room and heard the sound of someone bathing. I could hear the sound of water. I saw a small ventilator opening into my room, which was covered with a net curtain only. I pulled up my computer-table chair and climbed up to see who it was. To my luck, she had finished with her bath."

He sighed and I gathered how disappointed he must have felt. But continued nonetheless, "Then I put my chair back and lied down to sleep. I was thinking of ma'am continuously. The question that was revolving like earth in my mind was why she was taking a bath at that time? But then a thing clicked in my mind: she will definitely take a bath in the morning before going to college.

"I didn't sleep that night, waiting for the sound of water . The remaining night I spent sitting near the bathroom on the floor. I kept waiting but no sound of water reached me. I was so disappointed.

"I left for college and was waiting for her to come and start the lecture. She came for the sixth lecture and was looking more beautiful than the previous night. She was wearing a red-coloured sari. Despite the fact that I was a sincere student, looking at her had taken away all my sincerity. I could not concentrate on the lecture, and was busy imagining my teacher without her sari. She kept asking if somebody had any questions; but how could I ask her what time she would go for bath?"

I chuckled, not so much at the question, but the excitement with which Aadi was narrating the whole thing. He ignored me and carried on, "The day ended with great difficulty because I was very excited to see ma'am.

"Again, it was 8:00 pm in the evening and I was waiting for her to move for dinner. I had already decided I would not miss my chance that day. If she didn't leave her room, then I would also stay back. I didn't want to miss the opportunity at any cost. And the same thing happened – she did not go for dinner. Then around 11:00 p.m., I heard some noise of water in the bucket. I was ready with my chair to climb on. I could see everything clearly from within the net. She was in her night suit and took her clothes off one after the other. My eyes did not blink for a single second. She was having bath in the shower. Her body assets were shivering, while she was rubbing her assets with soap. I had already switched off my light so that she couldn't see me. She had no idea that someone else was watching her.

"I cannot forget how beautiful she was even in my dreams."

"Oh my god, Aadi. You are nuts. You didn't tell me any of this when we were in college, yaar.

"Of course, man! What do you expect? I was scared."

"So, you saw her for just that one day?" Even I was curious now.

He replied with a twinkle in his eyes, "Nope. Around fifteen days after that, I didn't sleep. Every night, I used to see her.

"Then, one day while I was watching her when she was taking a bath, enjoying the live show, I began thinking on how I had come to like her. Or I can say I was in love with her. I was lost somewhere in planning my future with her, and didn't see the honey bee coming closer. I tried to blow it off but again it came to disturb me. I was busy watching the live porn movie and suddenly it bit me on my nose, and I ended up shrieking 'F@#k!' without realising that she could hear me.

"When I turned towards her again, rubbing my nose, I saw her looking up at the window. Out of nervousness, I got down from the chair and put it back in the right place. The bee-sting-pain was nothing in comparison to the anxiety that had come to grip me. I had a feeling that she would definitely complain to the dean and then the dean would call my parents.

"That's when I heard a knock on the door, and I was expecting that. I opened the door with one hand on my cheek for safety, just in case she thought of slapping me. It was her, dressed in her night suit."

"As soon as she saw me, she shouted, 'What happened?'"

"I stammered a 'Nothing, ma'am' quickly."

"She didn't look too angry. She asked me, 'I heard your shriek in the bathroom. Is everything alright?'"

"I was relaxed at the thought that she was still unaware of what I had been doing. I put my hand down from the face and she saw my swollen nose.

"She came closer and asked me, 'What has happened to your nose?'

"I answered quickly, 'Nothing, ma'am. I was just using the toilet and a honey bee bit me.'

"She laughed out loudly, 'Oh my god! Your nose is looking like a bread *pakoda*.'

"I smiled and apologised for using the slang word so loudly. She just smiled and asked me if I had put any ointment on it yet. I shook my head at which her expression changed suddenly. She held my hand and literally dragged me into her room mumbling, 'If you didn't put some medicine on this, it will trouble you.' She opened her first aid box, put on some ointment on a cotton ball, held my chin with her left arm and with the right arm she fixed that cotton on my nose. And I fell in love with her again. I had no worry for my *bread pakoda* nose. I wanted to express how much I loved her, but couldn't.

"I left the room after the medication by the most beautiful doctor of the world. And next day I didn't attend the college because of my swollen nose. The whole day I was missing ma'am and decided not to sneak in on her anymore. I was in love with her."

He looked so much in love even while talking about it, I was wondering how I wasn't able to see through it during college days.

"In the evening, she came to my room. I was ecstatic and she was apologising for disturbing me. How could I have told her it was a pleasure to see her! She asked me how my nose was, and I said it was cured. After all, her hands had touched it, even if indirectly.

"Then she told me she wanted to check for herself. She came closer and just as I was tempted to tell her how much I loved her, her phone started ringing. It was kept on my bed, and the screen flashed 'Jaanu calling'. Her smile on reading the name was incomparable to anything that I had ever seen. She abruptly got up and told me, 'Okay Aadi, get well soon. I have to go.' And she vanished.

"All my dreams had been broken by the "jaanu". At that moment, I was even tempted to see her again from the window and make the video to sell in the college. Though I saw her every night from that little window, I dropped the idea of making a video. After a year, she shifted her room."

I was listening to all of it patiently and the moment he finished, his sad expression was too much to handle and I broke into uncontrollable laughter. Hahahahahaha.

Aadi looked agitated, "Neev, don't laugh! I really loved her yaar."

"Oops, sorry 'jaanu'," I teased him and broke into a fresh fit of laughter.

Aadi got up with a smile and said, "You are mad, Neev. I think you should rest now, enough laughter at my expense."

I had not yet had my fill with him, so continued with my joke, "As you wish, Aadi jaanu".

This time even he could not control and joined me in what would be the most memorable laughter session between the two of us after years.

In the meanwhile, I had half a mind of discussing those boys who were bothering Aashi in the morning, but then I felt that it wasn't the right time.

Post-dinner, I revised my definitions of "death rate" in order to clear Aashi's doubt. More so to not feel under-confident with the way she had been asking questions in front of the entire class.

Next day at exact 9:00 am after finishing my breakfast, I was standing at the main gate waiting for both of them. I could hear aunty shouting at Aadi and Aashi to be quick because I was waiting.

They both came and we started for college. I was slightly worried for the lecture in Aashi's class.

I entered the class and wrote the topic "DEATH RATE" on the board.

I turned around and announced that those students who had a problem in this topic can ask their queries.

Aashi got up and asked the same question again, "Could you explain this topic in a manner that I could get it?"

I felt all my work on the topic had gone waste. From the way she said it, it seemed she had not understood anything at all. I opened the book and began to teach the topic all over again.

After finishing the topic, I asked if there were any more doubts, addressing it specifically to Aashi.

"I have understood it now, sir. Thanks for co-operating."

"It's my duty to guide you. What's there to thank me about?"

Aashi promptly said, "That's true."

Such behaviour was surprising. The whole class didn't say anything; it seemed Aashi used to do things to tease teachers earlier as well.

Next day again Aashi did the same thing; she teased me a lot over the topic I was teaching. Every time, at every question she wanted perfection from me.

Sometime she used to comment from the back, sometimes she talked loudly with the girls, sometimes she ate her tiffin in between the class and when I shouted at her, she started arguing with me.

I didn't know why she was doing that.

Things went on in a similar fashion for a month. But at the end of it, I had two things in my pocket - my first salary and the habit of writing a diary. The former enabled me to pay the rent and the latter helped me vent my feelings out. I used to pen down my daily routine in that diary. Still I used to spend nights thinking of my dad. I had stopped thinking of my future and started living life in the present. Due to my introvert nature, I had only two friends in Agra: Aadi and Aliya. However, with them also, I didn't share my feelings, or the pain which was buried in my heart. I only shared things which made them happy. Life was tasteless, as if I was having food without salt.

Sometime I also used to think about Aashi; as to why she behaved like that with me. If she had any problem with me regarding living at her house, she could have simply said so and I would have shifted to some other place.

The other reason could have been those boys. I was a total failure that day. I could only hope that she would understand me some day and stop hating me.

4

HARYANVI CHORA AND CHINKY JI

When I got my first salary, I went to the market and purchased new clothes for myself. I took Aadi's help in this task. This newfound feeling of independence made me more confident. As usual, three of us were moving for college. I had never discussed my friction with Aashi with Aadi. I also noticed that those boys didn't utter a syllable in front of Aadi. It might be because Aadi had good contacts, so maybe they were scared of him.

I had my second lecture in Aashi's class. I entered the class and repeated the same questions which I was sure Aashi would stand up to: "If someone has any problem regarding the topic we discussed yesterday, please go ahead and ask me. As usual, Aashi asked the question. Every day. I was more petrified with the questions she asked and not so much from the most intelligent of students.

I patiently explained the concept for a brief while and subsequently gave them a numerical to solve. While everyone was busy solving the numerical, Aashi was busy fidgeting with her fountain pen. I didn't disturb her, as I didn't want to argue with her again. She was the single student using fountain pen, but I ignored and carried on with the lecture.

Another day was over, that too a Friday. I had planned to have full rest over the weekend. Nevertheless, when I reached home and removed my brand new white shirt, I saw my back smeared with blue ink. I could very well guess who could have done this – that vampire Aashi. I was very angry, but knew well that I couldn't say anything to her.

I was not able to fathom why Aashi was hell bent on doing all this. Neither did I share anything about my shirt with Aadi, nor complained to Aashi when she came to offer me dinner.

On Saturday morning, I myself cleaned the ink spot from my shirt. I bought some washing powder of good quality and started rubbing the ink off. Since the bathroom was too small for washing, I was doing so on the terrace.

Suddenly Aashi came to the roof for some work, and when she saw me washing the shirt, she started laughing. I saw her once; my blood was boiling inside after seeing her behave like that. If Aashi had not been Aadi's sister, I would have killed her. But I managed and concentrated on my work, ignoring her altogether.

At work, all other students were comfortable with me, except Aashi who was adamantly creating troubles for me every day. The semester was nearing its end and I had planned to change my section because of Aashi. There was only a month and a half left.

I was sitting in the staff room with Aliya after finishing my lectures. As usual, she was discussing her daily problems and now she had her latest topic concerning her boy friend that he had not wished her on her birthday.

Suddenly, Aadi came to the staff room. Aliya excused herself so that we could talk comfortably. But Aadi stopped her and requested her to sit and give us company. We were discussing the college environment and the general way in which things were going when Aadi started flirting with Aliya.

"Hey, Neev, I forget to tell you something I had come to meet you about."

"Tell me, Aadi, what happened?"

"I will have to leave for Delhi from college itself for some university work. Therefore, you have to do me a favour. I am going to be travelling with Dean Sir. Can you pick my bag from home and bring it to the railway station. I have talked to mom, and she has packed my bag.

"Yeah, of course. But I have not seen the route to the station."

"No worries about that. You can take my bike and come with Aashi; she will tell you the way."

I agreed, but somewhere was also worried hearing Aashi's name.

When we told Aashi the plan ater leaving college, she asked me if I knew how to drive a bike.

"Yes, of course."

"Great! I don't like to ride with learners."

I didn't quite understand what she meant, and let it pass. At home, aunty was ready with Aadi's bag. But along with the bag, she handed over a list of things that had to be bought on the way back home. I took the bike and asked Aashi to sit.

"And don't worry, I know how to drive," I added before revving the bike up.

Aashi merely chuckled. That's when I got to know that Aashi also could smile. As far as I remember, it was her first time in front of me. I drove the bike at more than 80 km/hr. Aashi was giving me instructions for the route; the station was around five kilometres from home. Aashi warned me many a times to drive slowly, but I didn't give any importance. I just had one excuse – Aadi was waiting for us. And she had to accept it.

We reached station before time, Aadi told us to leave immediately as the train was late. We moved from there.

I asked Aashi to tell me the route again, because I was bad at remembering roads.

She commented, "You can't remember the routes, then how do you manage to teach in the college?"

I didn't like the way she said it, so retorted, "Listen, there is a lot of difference in remembering roads and teaching."

"Okay, then, go on your own. I don't want to sit on your bike."

I could only mumble slowly, "Fuck". But added in a very pleasant tone, "Okay, we could fight on this topic at home; cooperate here with me.

A little away from the station, there was a shop where all the things on aunty's list would be available, or so Aashi told me and asked me to stop and wait. She moved in to bring the things and I was waiting on the road with the bike. After a little over fifteen minutes she came out of the shop and shouted, "Hey, help me!"

I locked the bike and reached the shop. I took the bag which had been put right next to her.

When I was getting down from the stairs, suddenly a man shouted "*pakdo chor*".

I put the bag down and ran towards Aashi, she was laughing at me and was showing the genuine bag to me.

I apologised to that person and turned to Aashi to tell her, "If you were not my student, I would have killed you long ago."

Ignorant of my agitation, she again laughed out loudly.

I didn't react, but deep inside, I was not agitated at her activities and pranks; I could merely smile.

I always noticed one thing about Aashi: she never addressed me with words like sir, *bhaiya* or anything else. She just abruptly began talking. She was sitting at the back of the bike, with one hand on my shoulder and the bag in the other. I liked the way she put her hand on my shoulder.

She suddenly asked me to stop the bike at a medical store. She told me to get one medicine from the store, as she held the bags.

I asked her which medicine she wanted, and she said any painkiller would do.

I got the medicine and gave it to her, "Why don't you see a doctor? I have seen you complain of this pain so many times.

"Thanks for the suggestion, but I think you should concentrate on driving," was her prompt reply.

This time, I drove slowly.

When we reached home, Aashi didn't say anything to me and moved inside. After talking to Aadi s dad for a few minutes, I went into my room. That night, memories of my father disturbed me and I slept off without having eaten a morsel.

Next morning, I was standing at the gate, waiting for Aashi as usual. Aashi came and we moved towards college. I felt that after the previous day's bike ride, we were a bit friendly with each other. Also because she smiled whenever we had eye contact. I was happy to see this.

We were about to reach college when I saw those boys again. I was slightly scared because Aadi was not with us. I was sure that they'd comment something again, and I didn't know how to react.

I was praying to god to give me some strength. Even Aashi looked scared, maybe more uncomfortable because she knew that I would not to do anything.

And suddenly, one of the boys – dark-complexioned, short and muscular – shouted, *"Jaaneman, aaj to akele aayi ho"*.

We thought ignorance would be the only way to be saved, so we did not react at all.

Now, another boy shouted, *"Aaj to mausam bhi suhana hai"*.

I didn't know why he would say such a thing on such a hot day. Meanwhile, Aashi was looking at me, perhaps waiting for me to react.

So as not to disappoint her and me again, I somehow managed to say, *"Chalo be taporiyon!* Get out of here.*"*

One of the boys from the group said, *"Oho,* the hero has finally spoken up".

Another one added, "Come to the *taporis* once and a get a taste of it".

By this time, we had entered the campus and were unable to hear more comments.

I was tense as it all had happened again.

While I was taking Aashi's class later on, I saw that she was not paying attention. She put her head down on the bench. In between the lecture, once she looked up and I saw her eyes –complete red and brimming with tears.

I couldn't stop myself and asked, "What happened to you Aashi?" As expected, she didn't answer.

One of the girls sitting next to her spoke up instead, "She has been like this since morning."

I again asked, "Aashi, are you having that headache again?" She shook her head to say no.

Then what happened to you?"

She didn't answer. And I was sure she was behaving like this because of those boys. So I also didn't probe any further.

The entire day, I was feeling terrible and thinking the way to get out of this trouble, but I failed to find a solution.

I was not paying attention to what Aliya said; I didn't share anything with her. She asked me many times if there was something wrong with me, but I didn't discuss.

When it was time to go back home, I was again thinking about those boys and how I'd face them in front of Aashi and other people in college.

Aashi came to the staff room at the right time; she still had fear on her face. I tried to talk to her, but she didn't respond. I think she was also scared of what the boys would do now.

We were about to reach the main gate of the college; my heart was beating fast and I was praying to god with every heartbeat. I didn't like to fight, I didn't want to harm someone, and I did not want to be hurt myself. I was also concerned because I was a teacher in the college and I was expected to show decency in the presence of students. I was a respectable person, not a loafer like those *taporis*. If I fought with those boys, it would be against my image and my profession. I did not know what to do.

After putting the first step out from the gate, the only thing I saw was those boys standing in the front. They were same in number, four.

Aashi kept looking back at me every now and then. One of the boys shouted from the distance, "The hero is here!"

And the one right next to him added in the same cheesy tone, "The heroine is with him."

Aashi warned me not to say anything and to just move on. I was mumbling.

As we went nearer, a boy grabbed Aashi's bag and pulled towards himself. Aashi started crying loudly. I saw Aashi and then told those boys, "Why are you irritating a student, *bhai*?"

One of the boys, who looked the heaviest among all, said, "In the morning, we were *taporis;* now we are *bhais*!" He didn't stop at that; he went ahead and put a hand on Aashi's cheek, saying, "*Jaan,* don't cry".

Many girls were standing and witnessing all this, but none had guts to say anything.

And this time, I couldn't stop myself.

I pulled his hand and gave him a slap on his face.

Aashi was shocked to see this. I realised that all the girls had made a circle around us all so that none of the four boys could escape. I saw this as a form of support.

Another boy came from behind me and hit me on my shoulder with a belt. I moved towards him and picked up the same belt to hit him on his face with it, thrice. The first boy came from the back and beat me continuously on my shoulder with his belt.

The two other boys were standing next to their bikes and after seeing me beating their friend, they put their bike on stand. One boy pushed me on the road and I fell. I saw some broken bits of bricks placed near the corner of the road; I picked one brick and hit that boy with it. It hit him on his forehead and he began bleeding profusely. Shortly after that, he fell flat on the road. I was scared. Two boys approached me – one with a chain and the other with a belt. I didn't have anything else except one brick which I had thrown towards the boy who was carrying a chain in his hand. Similarly, he too fell on the road.

Aashi was shouting, "Just kill them all; *maaro saalon ko*".

The remaining two boys saw their two friends lying on the road. They stopped fighting and picked them up and put them on the bike before leaving.

Aashi had an indefinable smile on her face; she just ran towards me and kissed on my cheek and said, "You are awesome". I was thanking the bricks; otherwise they would have easily killed me.

All the girls standing there started clapping and cheering. Aashi realised the sheer number of people around and shied away. She asked me to move for home. Aashi's face brightened like a tube light and when we moved a few away from the crowd, she asked me, "Why did you fight?"

I answered, "To see this smile on your face." She smiled and said nothing.

She asked me after a few seconds, "Did you get hurt? Is it paining?"

I said, "No, not that much."

"That means it is paining."

"Yeah, but it is nothing compared to the pain that life has given me in the past few months. Aashi went quiet again.

After reaching home, I took the way to my room. I didn't speak anything about the fight to aunty and uncle.

After sometime, somebody knocked at door. It was uncle. I welcomed him in and offered him a chair.

The first words he said were, "Thank you, beta".

"Don't say this, uncle ji. What have I done?" I didn't want him to thank me.

"No beta, it's a lot for us. … Are you hurt?"

"No uncle, I am fine."

Again there was a knock, and this time it was Aashi with aunty.

As they came in, aunty suddenly asked, "Are you alright, beta? You fought with so many people."

"No, really I am fine. I don't get hurt so easily, all thanks to your *aloo gobhi.*"

All of us laughed at this together, while Aashi blushed.

In both of them, I could see my parents.

I looked towards Aashi. She was standing quietly but in her eyes I could read many things.

After a little conversation, they all left the room.

I was penning down the day's incident in my diary; I was thinking many things about Aashi and jotting them all down in the diary. I was thinking about the moments I spent with Aashi the previous day. Aashi had kissed on my cheek, did not want to sit on the bike yesterday. The way she made a fool out of me with the wrong bag. I was smiling to myself after remembering those moments.

I was smiling after a long time. I think I had started liking Aashi.

I was taking rest in my room when the door to my room flung open – Aadi. He shouted after seeing me, "My Haryanvi *chhore, tu to ghana sher nikla.* I had never thought you capable of doing such a thing." Before I could utter a single word, he hugged me and said thank you.

"Shut up, Aadi. Don't say thanks and insult our friendship."

Aadi smiled and said, "During college days, Neev, you always hated to fight. But what happened to you today?"

Aadi knew me too well for me to make things up. "Aadi, I still hate to fight. But I couldn't stop myself when they crossed the limit."

"Oh, well really, you did a great job, Neev. Do you know what happened to those boys?"

"No, yaar. How are they? I was an animal at that time."

"Oh yeah, you were. One of the boys got close to fifty stitches and the other one around twelve.

I was shocked, "How do you know this?"

"They called me to apologise; they are afraid of you."

"Oh, my god."

"You are the new don here," he chuckled. I joined him.

"So your work at Delhi is finished?" I asked him.

"Yeah, it was completed."

"Neev, can you do me a favour?" Aadi said.

"Oh, come on! Don't say that. What favour?"

"Neev, I really love her."

"Stop it. I know your love, may I know how much love you have at present?"

"Hmm, I think it's about five who I really love and seven are just time pass."

"Oh my god, how could you handle all of them?" I played along.

"Neev, my friend, it's an art. You'll not understand."

"Oh art! So you are an artist now!"

Both of us laughed a hearty laugh.

I told him straight away, "But for your kind information, Aliya already has a boyfriend."

"So what? She will leave him when she'll feel the warmth of my love."

"Ah, great! I will see what I can do for you '*jaanu*'."

He laughed with me, but the spark in his eyes could not be missed.

"Hey Neev, do you remember the day when all hostel boys had gone to buy sex?" he asked conspiratorially.

"Yeah I remember. You had some tragedy there too?"

"Don't talk like that, man! You were out of station due to some exams during that time."

"Yeah, I had gone to Delhi for an exam. So what happened exactly?"

He started telling me, "It was time for the fifth semester. Arjun Singh had newly shifted to my room. I didn't know where in hell he heard about "Chinky". He told me there was a group of girls who had newly come to Hotel Spine. That hotel was famous for these things only. He told me that the leader of that group was Chinky.

"She arranged for the room, food, wine, and set the amount of money to be paid. I was excited after hearing all this. Without thinking anything else, I asked Arjun where could one find Chinky?

"Arjun told me that she was always available at the same hotel. So we decided to go the next day, without saying anything to anyone else in the college. The most awaited day of our lives had come. We bunked our college and reached the hotel around 2:00 p.m. We had a thousand rupees each in our pocket and Arjun felt that amount was enough for the place. I had managed this amount by selling all my semester books. I thought I would read books by borrowing them from someone.

"When we entered the hotel, Arjun asked in very soft voice, "We want to meet Chinky". The man at the reception showed his fingers to the right. At the right of him, there was a room. We moved towards the room; both of us were nervous because it was our first time. We knocked at the door and a beautiful girl around twenty-five years old came to open the door. After seeing that beautiful lady, we were sure that we would achieve the goal definitely."

I was surprised to hear that Aadi had gathered the guts to do such a thing. But my reverie was cut short as he continued, "We asked that girl if we could meet Chinky ji. She told us she was the person and asked what we wanted.

"I was slightly nervous to speak up, but that Arjun was behaving like a child. He asked her directly that if she could arrange girls for sex. To my surprise, she agreed and called us in, without a moment of hesitation. That room was a hall divided into little rooms; right in the middle of the hall was a sofa set. We were sitting on that and Chinky sat right next to us." Aadi seemed to be enjoying the moment of narrating it as well.

"Then what happened?" I asked him to go on.

"The, she asked us what sort of girl we wanted and Arjun was so desperate that he said anyone would do. I cut him short and told her that we need someone between twenty to twenty-three years of age. She said okay and clapped her hands thrice. Around six girls immediately came in front of our eyes. Neev, brother, I can't define their beauty; they all had body parts which were really admirable. Chinky introduced all those girls by their name and their rates, Sita- five hundred rupees, Sangita- four hundred and fifty rupees, etc.

"We chose two perfect girls from them. Chinky fixed eight hundred rupees each, including food, wine, and room. Both of us gave all the money in advance. The girls held our hand to take us into the respective rooms. We entered the room; it was air-conditioned, and all the food and drinks were already arranged."

"Then what happened?" I was curious.

"Brother, she closed the door and I was so excited. The name of my girl was Sita; she was the most beautiful among all. I was happy to see that I would lose my virginity to a girl like her. Not a 'good' girl, but beautiful. I guess I could compromise that much. She was sitting right next to me and her hand was on me. I was nervous and I told her that it was my first time with her, that's why. She realised the reason for my nervousness. I tried to show off and told her, 'No, I am not nervous.' I told her in a confident voice, so that she doesn't feel that I have zero experience. She came close to me and started kissing on my cheek. And before I knew, she suddenly started smooching. When she was smooching, I heard Arjun's voice. I was lost in better things to notice what he was saying.

"Slowly, she began unbuttoning my shirt and jeans, and when I began to loosen her clothes, she stopped me for a while. Dude, how could I have stopped myself from doing that? I continued and everything was going good. But as usual, something unexpected happened. I had never thought this could happen with me. The upper portion of Sita was just as a normal woman would have, but when I reached the lower portion, I was shocked. Shocked is an understatement; I was about to faint. How could this happen with me? She was not a she; she was not a he."

I couldn't control my laughter at this. Here I was waiting for Aadi to narrate something interesting, and he came up with this!

He stopped me with a wave of his hand and continued, "I shouted, who are you? She said pleadingly that she is Sita. I could only say 'fuck you, Sita' at that point. I didn't want this. And then I got to know why Arjun was shouting.

"I put on all my clothes and moved out of the room, to meet Chinky. I saw Arjun already arguing with her. I asked Arjun if the same thing had happened with him also. He said yes. We both were angry and asked Chinky why did she do such a thing with us. She just smartly said, 'You had chosen them yourself. And if you say another word to me, I will call the police.'"

"Ulta chor kotwal ko daante!" my heart said,

"Yes, absolutely. We wanted our money back. And the moment we uttered that, two bouncers came to us and picked our collars to throw us out of the hotel. We both kept sitting opposite the hotel entrance for a long time, thinking what we could do. And finally, we decided to get back to college." He finished, as if still pained by the loss of those eight hundred rupees.

I was shocked, "Oh my god! You were fooled by Chinky, your money taken, and you were thrown out of the hotel... and you couldn't do anything to her."

"What could we have said, Neev. I just told you what the situation was."

"You didn't say anything to Arjun?"

"Oh hell, I made him pay the penalty. Next time in Delhi, he paid all the bills for our sexual escapades," Aadi winked.

"So you went for it again?"

"Yeah, many a time. But after facing this, we used to confirm in the beginning itself, whether she was a girl or not."

Both of us laughed out loud.

I further added after much thought, "Aadi, I want to appreciate Chinky's skills."

Aadi made a face in mock anger and told me, "Neev, don't make fun of us like this."

We laughed heartily, after which Aadi bade me good night and left, leaving me waiting for Aashi

to come and give me dinner.

I was thinking of Aashi when there was a knock on the door. I was sure she was Aashi definitely.

I opened the door and faced somebody I had wished for.

I welcomed Aashi and took the dinner from her hand. Today she had some special glow on her face. I hadn't seen anything like this before.

She did not discuss anything with me about the day and left the room.

I was having dinner and again there was a knock, I left my food and opened the door. It was again Aashi.

"What happened, Aashi?"

She took out a lotion from her night suit pocket. Then I noticed how pretty she looked in that sky blue night suit.

As she handed over the bottle of that lotion, I asked her what it was for.

"Sorry for disturbing you at this time; I should come later after you have finished your dinner."

"No, no! It's okay, Aashi. Tell me."

"You can put this lotion at places where you are feeling pain," she said slowly. Saying this, she left.

I continued with my dinner. While eating, I was thinking of each family member in this house and how they had become almost like family for me. I was getting over my pain. My memories of my dad were getting weak to remember. In the daytime, I did not remember my dad, but in the evening when I used to go for sleep, I felt the pain of his having left me alone in this big world. I was penning down all my activities that had happened that day. And yet again, I could not stop myself from writing more about Aashi. Sometimes I felt I had something in my heart for Aashi, but when I thought of her family, I let go of all these thoughts automatically. After writing the diary, I got up to close the only window in my room, which faced towards Aashi's room. There, almost instinctively, I looked at Aashi;s window, don't know why?

The more unusual thing, Aashi was standing near the window and was looking towards my room. When I had an eye contact with her, she started doing some signs.

I didn't understand and asked her to do it again.

She picked up a paper and a black marker from her room and started writing on it.

I was waiting patiently for her to complete her writing.

As soon as she wrote, she showed the paper. "Did you put the lotion?" I nodded a yes, although I still had to put the lotion after closing the window. If I would have said no to Aashi, she would have felt bad.

I closed the window.

I was thinking of Aashi and the lotion, and why was she so caring for me that particular day. It could be because I had saved her today. After this incident, it became clear that Aashi's earlier rude behaviour with me was just because of those boys. At that time, my not reacting or saying anything to those boys must not have hurt her.

I was tired, so the lotion stayed on the side table and I slept off. I was too tired to do anything.

There was something different in the way I was feeling for Aashi... the thought about her made me very relaxed. I wondered if this was love. It was a beautiful feeling which made the entire environment beautiful. When she was with me, I prayed to God that I needed her in my life. I wanted to tell her about my helplessness, but I couldn't say anything. I knew only one thing – Aashi was changing my life.

5

APRIL – THE MONTH BEGAN WITH LOVE

Generally it is said that there is no season of love. It can be anytime…but for certain things, time is essential. For me, love came in the month of April.

Next morning, when I got up for college, my back and shoulder was paining. I couldn't move my shoulders at all. It was paining due to the fight, I presumed. After having breakfast, we all moved towards college.

The pain was causing me a lot of stress. Aashi noticed me but she didn't say anything as Aadi was there. Aadi was asking me about the same lotion to put on the body and this ensured that Aashi had not discussed the lotion with someone in the family. I maintained the decorum and didn't tell Aadi that Aashi had already given me that lotion.

We reached college and all three of us moved to our respective places. I was stepping in the staffroom and Aliya commented something. There were around two or three teachers sitting in the staff room, but they did not notice things did by Aliya, as she always talked much.

I said while taking a seat, "Stop it, Aliya. I am not a stud or anything."

"Oh, don't be modest. Your name is on everyone's lips in Agra.

This time I didn't notice her and opened a book of my subject.

Aliya also didn't force me to talk.

After spending an hour, I moved out for my lecture in Aashi's class. I spoke on my topic and was about to write something on the black board, but suddenly my nerves stretched and I felt a shooting pain in my shoulder. Although I wrote on the board what I had to, the pain could be seen on my face. Today I was observing Aashi; she was not doing anything like arguing, asking stupid questions, as she usually does. But she was looking at me continuously, even unblinkingly I thought, I didn't know why.

Anyhow, I completed my day and I realized the mistake of not putting the lotion on my body given by Aashi.

Upon reaching home, I went straight to my room and lay down, because I was suffering immense pain. Aashi brought lunch.

She didn't say anything and came inside. While she entered, I was watching her face. I oculd read anger and wondered what had happened. She put the lunch on the table and came near the door, and she locked it from inside.

I asked her, "What happened?" I was a bit tense as to why she had bolted the door.

She shouted, "What do you think of yourself?"

"Nothing Aashi, but why you are saying this?" I was baffled with her tone and words.

"Do you think I am stupid?" She was very angry.

I mumbled slowly, "There is nothing to make me think you are stupid, dear. You are a nice girl."

"Then why didn't you use that lotion when I asked you to do that? You know, I sneaked it out of my mom's room, without telling her, just because of you."

Then I understood the reason behind her wrath, "Sorry Aashi, I forgot yesterday."

Her expression changed from bad to worse, "So you lied to me?"

"Yeah, Aashi; I am sorry." I should not have lied to you.

She looked at me in anger, and said, "Put that lotion on the places where you are feeling pain right away."

"Aashi, I will put it after you leave."

"Nope, I said just now. Otherwise, I will not leave you."

Okay, okay. I have to loosen my shirt for that; just look in the opposite direction.

I applied the medicine and asked Aashi to turn.

She quickly ordered, "Okay, now I am leaving. Before sleeping in the night, put it once again."

"Definitely," I said, scared.

She left the room. And just after she had gone, my heart melted like wax. I don't know why, but I wanted to cry as much I could.

I was thinking of her, and how she had been as caring as my father.

Tears ran down my cheeks. I used to think something else about Aashi, but my eyes moved towards that lotion on the table and again my tears rolled down.

I knew I was getting sentimental just because no one had cared for me like this ever in my life. I don't know how mothers care for their children.

Anyhow, I managed myself to think something else and did not think anymore, to get back to normalcy.

The remaining days passed by and I was waiting for Aadi to come. In the evenings, Aadi used to come sometimes to talk.

One evening, I heard Aadi shouting. I opened my window and saw Aadi calling me to come down.

I got down from the room and Aadi told me that he was going to show me a bit of the city. Agra at night.

We both chuckled and I sat on his bike.

I was still feeling a bit pain on my shoulder but I thought this would change my mood.

I saw Aashi watching me from the kitchen.

Aadi drove me to "Raja Mandi", a famous bazaar in Agra. But it's difficult to say what it is famous for. It's because most of the Agra girls come here for most of the things can be easily bought. For Aadi, it didn't matter what things were available in the market; he was busy checking out the girls.

I was frustrated, a complete hour was over, but he was still standing near the ice cream shop and watching girls. I was also feeling slight pain in my shoulders all along.

I asked him, "Aadi, what we are doing here?"

He said in a very crispy manner, "We are seeing the most beautiful creations of god."

"Aadi, you know I don't like this."

"Neev, that's why I've brought you here. I want to bring about some changes in you. I want to see you a happening person. Who loves to roam outside, who loves to talk to girls."

"Aadi, I am fine yaar. I don't like all this."

"Oh god! What kind of friend you are? You know Neev, this place every boy enjoys, but you dislike this place."

"Aadi, I am feeling uncomfortable here."

"You are so unpredictable for a boy; almost behaving like girls. Okay let's go home."

"Sorry for spoiling your mood."

"Oh come on!"

Within a minute, we left for home.

I saw Aashi working in the kitchen. She was watching from the window, situated exactly in front of the gate.

I wished Aadi good night and left for my room. I lay there, resting in my bed and thinking about the afternoon.

Suddenly, I heard a knock on my door. It was dinner time, so I was sure it must be Aashi. And I was right.

She put my dinner on the table and asked me, "What was the need to go out and waste time roaming when you still have body pain?"

"I didn't want to go, but I wanted to freshen up my mind. And how could I have said no to Aadi?"

"Okay, so how was your pain?"

"It's much better now; I am relieved by almost 80%."

"Great, use it once more before going to bed."

I said okay and she left the room.

I had taken my meal and was preparing to sleep. But for some reason, I wanted to see outside from the window.

I was standing near the window and looking at the window opposite. Aashi was standing near her window with a marker and a paper. She saw me and waved her hand.

I replied with a wave of my hand.

She suddenly started writing on the paper.

She wrote and displayed the paper towards me: "Lotion".

I knew I couldn't lie to her today and wrote, "No".

She looked angry and wrote on the paper, "Right now".

After reading the words, I remembered the afternoon. I moved from the window and put the lotion on my shoulder. I came back quickly towards the window; she was still waiting for me. I wrote, "Yes, I did" on the paper and showed to her. After that, we wrote good night to each other and moved away from our windows.

I was thinking of Aashi as I lay down. In addition, I knew, she was taking care of me because I had helped her. I dozed off to sleep, thinking of her.

Next morning, I went through my usual routine. We reached college. I was entering the staff room and I saw Aliya with her head down on the table. I came near her and asked her if she was okay.

She heard my voice, and looked up towards me. Her eyes were full of tears. Still she managed to say, "Yeah I am fine."

"Oh yes, you are. Tell me the truth, Aliya."

A fresh gush of tears rolled down her cheeks as she choked the few words out, "Neev, I broke up with my boyfriend yesterday."

"I am sorry to hear that, Aliya, but what happened?

"I was standing in the bookstore in Raja Mandi market and suddenly I saw him in that book store. When I moved towards him, I saw a girl standing with him. First I thought, the girl would be some sister or cousin. So to confirm whether he was true to me or not, I gave him a call.

"He picked up the phone and when I asked him where he was, he abruptly said he was in a meeting and would call me later. I disconnected the call. And then when he saw me, he said sorry and started justifying that the girl was just a friend.

"I didn't say anything and moved out of that place."

"Don't be upset for such a guy, Aliya. You deserve someone better and more loving."

"Yeah, Neev you are right."

She still had tears in her eyes. I could easily understand the pain that she was feeling, so I left her to herself.

Soon after, I moved for the lecture in Aashi's class. I noticed that unlike before, Aashi stayed quiet while I was teaching and was attentive; nor did she cross question unnecessarily or spoke to her friends. I was happy to see this. After finishing my lecture, I left for the library. It was not enough to study at home to prepare for the lectures.

While we three were going back home, suddenly Aadi spoke up, "Yaar Neev. Can you help me?"

"Yes, of course. Tell me how and I'll do it."

"Neev, Aashi has some problems in studying accounts, so she was asking me to talk to you. Can you teach her for a while after college at home?" Aadi spoke very gently.

"Yeah of course, Aadi. Needless to say. And Aashi, why were you feeling so shy to tell me this? Am I so strict?"

"No, it's not like that. So can I come to you at 8 p.m. in the evening, if you don't have any problem?"

"Yes, definitely. Anytime you wish."

"So Aashi, from today onward, Neev is your 'sir'. At home, too."

"Okay," Aashi said.

We reached home and went to our rooms. After a few minutes, Aadi came into my room and offered lunch. I was expecting Aashi, but didn't mention. Suddenly, I remembered about Aliya's break-up and discussed it with him.

"Oh my god, Aliya is so lonely now. I should do something for her," Aadi said.

"Are you mad? What can you do for her?" I chuckled at his excitement.

"I need to give her support at this time. She need someone's shoulder to cry on. Some shoulder she can later call her own."

"*Saale kamine, ye bol na ki ab tera rasta khali hai*. Now your way to her is clear," I knew him just too well.

Aadi chuckled and left the room.

That left me wondering that Aashi had fixed the dinner time for studying. I was worried as to when I'd get my dinner now. Beyond this, I was desperate to spend some time with Aashi, that I would have foregone dinner as well. I was happy for this new tuition, whether it paid or not. I was happy to have gotten a chance to spend some time with her.

At the same moment, I was afraid because of my feelings for Aashi. I was scared that I'd not be able to hide them; that won't be good.

At exactly 8 p.m., Aashi knocked on my door; I opened and asked her to come inside. The first question she asked was, "How is your pain?"

"Yeah, it is fine now. So tell me, what do you want to study?"

"Are you mad? Do you really feel I need tuition for accounts? You clear all my doubts in class itself," she said without hesitation.

"But Aadi was telling me you have some doubts…"

"Oh, that was a lie. Otherwise, how would I have gotten such a chance to talk to you?" She smiled.

"Talk? Why do you want to talk to me?" I was perplexed.

"Firstly, I want to say sorry to you. For misbehaving in class and hurting you."

"It's okay, Aashi. But I want to ask you why you did all those things in class with me?"

She looked at me in the eyes and said softly, yet confidently, "You know, earlier I didn't like you. The first time I saw you, you were crying in your room. The second impression, you were scared of those boys teasing me. I didn't quite like you. You were scared. I thought as a guy, should be strong enough to take care of girl."

I looked at her and stayed quiet; I didn't have anything to say to her.

After some time, she left the room. She had not even opened the book.

She continued coming to my room to 'study' for almost two weeks, but never once opened the book. I asked her to study something, but Aashi was stubborn. She never wanted to do things that others liked; she did what she felt like. In the meanwhile, Aashi had bought a new mobile and she had forced me to buy a new mobile too. After the initial reluctance, and a whole lot of pressure from Aashi's side, I gave in.

Every day, she used to come to my room and spend either 15-20 minutes, or sometimes an hour too. After going back from my room, she would bring dinner for me. We used to share all our thoughts with each other. Many a time, she had cried for my family. I knew somewhere inside my heart that I loved her. But on the outside, I didn't want to show this feeling. I was scared of Aashi, Aadi and his parents. If Aashi didn't feel what I felt for her, then she will be hurt. I didn't want to lose her; she was the closest and dearest to me now. I was happy and content with the way things were going.

Aashi had completed one year of graduation. The next day, Aashi's second year was to begin. She had cleared all her subjects with good marks. Aashi and I were wonderful friends now.

Also, due to 100 % result of the class in the past two semesters, I had been promoted and allowed to teach the second year students as well. Not just this, my salary had also been increased by eight thousand. Since I did not have any other expenses except the house rent, I used to save money and invest all the money in a bank. I had planned to buy a flat, after investing some money. Many a days we used to talk at night over phone.

Every moment that was spent with Aashi was recorded in my diary. I loved to write about her and she knew that I used to write about her. There were also times when she brought my dinner and sat and ate with me. Now, she had fixed one hour with me in the evening. When she came in, she locked the door from inside; in case any family member came into the room during that time, she'd act like a student, open all her books and start questioning me. I felt guilty at such times, but I enjoyed those moments too. I had no one to share my feelings with, other than Aashi. She used to act like my mother at times, a friend at others and even my dad sometimes. I could feel every relation in her. Aashi never used to hide anything from me. She knew I was a very emotional, possessive kind of person.

Sometimes Aashi spoke to me as if she loved me deeply. But when she realized this, she controlled herself. She knew, like me, that love was not possible between us. And I loved her for this understanding as well.

When she came to my room one day, she was upset at having had a fight with her friends in college. In between her non-stop, animated talk about the fight, she told me that her family had gone for a party and that no one else was home except me and Aashi. Since I was like a family member, I presumed they had no fear of leaving the girl alone at home with me. They had all faith. They knew I will take care of their house and Aashi, without saying anything.

I was listening to her when suddenly she stood up and said she had pain in her head. She also told me that this kind of pain happened once in 3-4 months, and that she would become normal after a while. She had not consulted any doctor about this despite my insistence from day one. I was scared to think what had happened to her. I remembered that everyone had gone for some party. That scared me more because I had no idea of any hospital or clinic nearby. I didn't even think that I had a mobile phone and I could contact anyone instantly.

I had tears in my eyes and Aashi was still lying on the floor in my room. I came near her, touched her cheeks, and said, "Wake up, Aashi. Open your eyes!" There was no response. I picked her in my arms and moved out of the room.

My heart had melted completely, tears were rolling down. I ran down the stairs, but uncle-aunty's room was locked. I put Aashi on the floor and said, "Baby, don't worry. I am just coming." I didn't even know if she could hear me.

I poured some water in a glass and ran back towards her. I sprinkled some water on her face, but again no response. Her eyes were closed and she was breathing very fast. I picked her in my arms again and started running towards the roof. They had linked roofs, so I planned to get down from the neighbours' house. I kept telling her, "Baby, don't worry; you will be fine."

I was repeating the same sentence. Till the time I reached the roof, my face was wet with tears. When I was climbing the stairs, my eyes fell on Aashi's face. She was still and my tears had also been falling on her face.

Suddenly, I heard her sweet voice, "I know I will be fine."

I looked at Aashi; her eyes were open wide and she was smiling. I put her down on the roof itself and she immediately started laughing loudly and shouting, "April fool".

I wiped all my tears in front of her, and without saying anything else moved down from the roof to my room. She was right behind me, shouting, but I paid no attention and locked my room from inside. She was standing outside my room and shouting, "Please, Neev. Open the door! I am sorry; I never imagined you'd get so serious."

I was crying in my room and just had one thing in my mind: there is no one who cares for me, who understands me and I was wrong about Aashi. She also does not care. I was crying aloud saying, "Leave me alone! Just for a joke, you made fun of me."

She shouted loudly, "Just open the door for once, then I will go."

"You have lost all respect for me; just get lost."

"Please open the door for once, Neev. Please."

I opened the door; within seconds she ran and hugged me tightly. After a few seconds, she removed her hands from the shoulders and holding my cheeks, began to smooch. She was kissing me all over my face. I was shocked and confused on how to react.

She moved a step back and said, "I love you, and I know you love me too."

"You are wrong, Aashi; I don't love you. It's your mistake. You are a beautiful girl; I will never find a girl like you, but try to understand."

"You know very well, Neev, how stubborn I am. I want you to say that you love me too."

I was feeling restless, "Aashi, you know about me very well. I don't deserve you, or your family. Your family is like god for me and I cannot break their trust like this. Your family had given me a place to live when I had nowhere to go; they helped me at every step; they allowed me to be a member of their family. They all have faith in me; moreover, Aadi has faith in me." I stopped to look at her serene face with tears rolling down her cheeks.

"And even if I love you, Aashi, I cannot let that surface. I can't hurt so many kind people."

Aashi came closer to me and hugged me again. I pushed her back. She pulled me and again she kissed me on my lips. She was damn crazy to make love to me. I don't know what kind of girl she is; I was talking to her and she was busy in kissing and giving hugs to me.

I was almost afraid of her now. I knew she was a crazy girl, and will not to listen me.

Suddenly, the doorbell rang. She ran towards the door saying excitedly, "Mummy-papa have come; call you later."

I called after her, "Listen, I don't love you."

As I watched her from the window, she ran towards the main gate.

After about fifteen minutes, she called me on my cell phone.

I picked up the phone and the very first thing she told me was, "Listen, Neev, while I was acting that I was unwell, I saw in your tears how much you love me. Every drop of tear screamed, 'I love you' for me and made me say the same. I don't care about what you think of your debt to my family or my brother, I want you to tell me that you love me *right now*."

At every second, I wanted to say "I love you, I love you…," but when I thought of everyone and everything else around me, I kept quiet. I disconnected the call without saying anything. I was crying sitting on my bed.

She called me up many times and at every call, I wanted to say, "Baby, don't worry. I love you."

After complete one hour, she sent a text, "Come near the window".

I didn't reply to this also; I knew she will not accept my ignorance and extract that hidden yes.

She was standing and had paper and marker in her hand. I thought she had realized her mistake.

I opened the window; I saw she was crying.

She wrote something and displayed to me – "Sorry".

I had a smile of contentment that she understood; I picked my paper and wrote, "It's okay".

This time, she had a smile on her face, but I was scared after seeing smile on her face. She again picked the things and wrote, "I love you."

I wrote, "I don't, sorry."

She wrote, "Okay, just see me."

I was scared, the way she had shown the paper to me.

I was seeing continuously towards her, without blinking the eyes. She had moved from her place for a while and came with a thing in her hand.

Due to some distance, I couldn't see that thing; it was too small. She was rubbing that thing on her wrist. I was confused, what exactly she was trying to do.

Suddenly, I saw a flash of red colour on her wrist.

Oh my god, it was blade and she was cutting her wrist.

I took my cell and called her in front of her; she was still rubbing the blade on her hand. I was scared if she cut her veins, then it would be dangerous. I knew she was mad enough to do anything.

She picked her phone from the table and threw it on the floor. I was frightened, puzzled and too nervous to react. She had created a big problem for me. I had my own values and principles; and on the other side, I had a girl who is madly in love with me. Who can change my life from tasteless to spicy. I knew very well that for me, she was the only hope to re discover my life.

I felt that I was getting greedy, but instead, I had someone's life at stake here, which was more important than moral values and principles. Her hand was full of blood by now.

I was begging her to stop, but she only wanted to hear that one thing from me.

Anyhow, with more courage and strength, I managed to pick my marker and a paper.

I wrote, "I love you forever."

After reading that, she started crying; seeing her, tears rolled down my eyes as well.

I wrote another quote on paper, "You are mad".

She replied by writing, "For you, baby."

She was still crying, so I wrote, "Stop crying. I am always yours."

She replied, "It's hurting, baby."

I couldn't stop myself after this and I opened my door. I got down the stairs. It was around 12:15 a.m. and all the lights were off. I was planning to go Aashi's room, to give some first aid and to make love to my first love.

There was nobody in the hall; I picked up my courage and reached her room. I knocked the door slowly; she opened the door and hugged me. The floor of her room was full of blood and her mobile lay broken on the other end. I was crying, so was she. I put my hands on her cheek and said, "I love you, baby. Don't ever do this in future. Promise me!"

"Promise love, but you promise one thing. Never leave me alone."

"Aashi, I will never leave you." At that moment, I promised to be with her, but forgot to take the same promise from her.

I took her hand in mine and kissed it. I saw a first aid box on the table; she would have known that I would come. I picked it from there and took out the cotton from it. I cleaned the wrist with an antiseptic solution; she was cringing with pain as I blew air to soothe her. The blade had almost reached the vein.

When I was done bandaging her wrist, I said, "Take care, baby. I have to go. If someone sees, me, then it will be trouble for us."

"Okay Neev, you should go. But give me a hug before you go."

I held her in my arms for a moment and kissed her on her forehead. As I was moving out of the room, she pulled me towards her bed. I fell flat on my back due to the unexpected pull; the very next moment, she was on me. Before I could push her off, she had loosened my shirt buttons and was kissing me all over the chest. She was mumbling, "Love me, Neev. Please love me."

I held her by the shoulders and put her below me. I kissed on her neck and face. I took off her t-shirt and began kissing her on her stomach. My hands were on the jeans now. I pushed off my pant and simultaneously pulled down her jeans. I forgot everything else and made love to her for three hours. I left the room after that.

She was standing at the window. She saw me and gave me a flying kiss.

The only thing I wanted to say to her was, "I love you, I love you, I love you…."

After spending a few more minutes, I signalled that she should go to sleep. It was 5 in the morning and within minutes, her parents would wake up.

I was in my bed, thinking about Aashi. I was scared for what I had just done.

I was nervous for my future, wondering if it will be with Aashi. What Aadi would think of me when he gets to know all this was a constant fear.

I was penning down everything and was lost in my dreams with Aashi.

I was worried about Aadi and then his parents; they had believed in me.

I was sure Aadi would come to hate me.

We are happy with our love but we are worried about moral values of our family. Society can't accept these relations. It always tries to create problems. But when love knocks at our door, we welcome it happily. When we start going on the way of love, we are ready to face every kind of problem. When we don't know any kind of ethics, morals, and society, customs... when we take birth and we die... The achievement is love. Love takes birth between birth and death and can't be defined easily. It has so many meanings at the same time.

Part-2

6

DREAM

In everybody's life, dreams play an important role.

When I woke up the next day, the first thing I did was to look outside for Aashi. I didn't find her anywhere.

How was she? Did she have problem with her wrist? What did she tell her parents about? It's obvious that they noticed the injury. She also didn't have any phone so I couldn't confirm.

We set out for college at the usual time. The bandage was still there on her wrist but I didn't enquire about that in front of Aadi. I was feeling a bit odd towards Aadi that day; there was a feeling of guilt.

When Aadi was with me, it was really awkward because I was in a relationship with Aashi and Aadi was unaware of it. He was really such a true friend, I was upset at betraying him like this. Despite the fact that I wanted to tell him everything, I couldn't. I had become greedy. If I told Aadi, then definitely I would have Aashi. "Lose Aashi"... these words made me weak. I couldn't have lost her at any cost. This conflict was creating trouble inside me.

Upon reaching college, I was sitting in the staff room and talking to Aliya. Nowadays, most of the time, she asked me about Aadi. I don't know why.

Suddenly, Aadi came to the staff room. Without disturbing both of them, I continued my reading and went out for my lecture after some time.

In the second year, I had the second lecture in Aashi's class. As I finished my teaching in the first section and headed towards Aashi's class, I was standing in front of the whole class, but I kept on staring at Aashi. Some of Aashi's best friends were smiling, making me wonder if they knew.

Still my eyes were on Aashi on the last bench.

When I finished my lecture and got back to the staff room, Aadi was still sitting right next to Aliya. This was ensuring me that Aadi would be successful very soon. I had not commented and again continued to work.

They moved out for a walk. Although Aadi asked me to join them, I denied. I didn't want to disturb their conversation in any manner.

It was time for us to go home and I was waiting outside the staff room for Aashi and Aadi. I saw Aadi coming, excited.

I asked him, "*Saale,* you look pretty happy. Seems you have won over the girl. *Chhori patali ke tanne?*" I wanted to ask Aadi whether he proposed to Aliya or not.

"Yes friend, I told her that I am in love with her and she has asked me to wait for some time," he told me.

"Hey, hey! Don't worry at all; she will definitely agree."

"Hope so, Neev."

Suddenly, we saw Aashi coming and stopped talking of Aliya.

On our way home, Aadi asked Aashi, "How is your hand?"

"It is fine now."

I did a bit of formality, to make the condition look real. "What happened to her hand, Aadi?"

"Oh nothing serious. She was trying on her new glass bangles when they broke and hurt her on the wrist."

"Oh, Aashi you should take care of yourself," I said in mock anger.

"Yes, in future I would take care while trying bangles," she said as she looked into my eyes with love.

We were about to reach home and suddenly a small puppy came in our way. Aadi hated dogs, he suddenly changed his way. But Aashi stupidly picked it up in her hand. I too love to play with puppies; I put my hand on him. Aadi was shouting, "It is so dirty; leave him on the road, Aashi."

"No, I will not. I will take it home," Aashi cooed.

"If you take it home, then I'll take some action. I will probably let both of you stay out of home."

I was hearing the conversation between them when suddenly Aadi said to me, "Neev, you tell her."

"What can I say to her?" I said.

"Just ask her to leave that puppy," Aadi really hated dogs.

I told her, "Aashi, it is not good. Please leave him." But in real, I wanted her to take it home.

"What are you saying, Neev? You had told me that you love dogs, and see he is so cute," she said sweetly.

"Yeah he is cute, but you should listen to your brother."

She looked at me, and then at Aadi and said, "Okay, as you wish. I am leaving him."

And she let that puppy go.

We reached home and went to our rooms. I was curiously waiting for my lunch and more than lunch, I was waiting for Aashi. Suddenly someone knocked at the door, but it was Aadi.

I welcomed and asked him to share the food. He came in and started sharing his views about Aliya. I noticed he was really in love with Aliya. He had tears in his eyes and he was telling me that he really loved her.

I was puzzled after listening to him. Earlier he used to do bragging while talking about other girls, and while talking about Aliya, he was quite simple and clear. I excitedly said, "Aadi, are you okay, or joking with me?"

"No Neev. Please believe me, I love her. I've left all my girlfriends."

He still had tears in his eyes. I gave him a hug and promised to talk about him to Aliya.

More than Aadi, I was worried about seeing Aashi; she did not even have her phone, so I could not communicate with her.

After spending a few more moments with me, Aadi left the room.

Later in the evening, I was waiting for Aashi to come. Exactly at 8 p.m., I opened my window to see her. The window was closed.

My heart was beating fast for Aashi, whether she would come or not. There was a knock on my door. I had goose bumps on my body. I opened the door; it was Aashi, my love, my angel.

She came inside, pushed the door with her leg, and hugged me. I mumbled slowly in her ear, "How is your hand, baby?"

"Now it's good, after giving you a hug."

I sighed slowly.

She had not let me go from her arms, and I was feeling very comfortable. It was like heaven to me. I asked her about her phone.

"I was dying to talk to you, baby. I have given my phone to one of my classmates for repairing; she will bring it tomorrow."

I made her sit on the bed, picked the books from her and put them on the table. I saw her hand, she had removed the cotton. I make myself comfortable and sat on the floor.

The injured hand was in my left hand and I was slowly putting my right hand on the injured place.

"What was the need to do this stupidity?"

"I didn't have any other option to make you speak out," she made a puppy face.

"You are a fool," I chided her.

"Who cares? I love you." She pulled me towards the bed and made me lie on her. I was sleeping on her body. She had put her hands on my back from inside the shirt. I was kissing on her neck and moving my hands all over her. She was mumbling, "I love you, I love you".

We just wanted to love each other, anyhow, all the time. She un-buttoned my shirt and started kissing me on the chest while her hands on my back pulled me closer towards her. Both of us didn't want to get separated from each other. We wanted to get closer to each other. We were crazy to make love to each other.

"Do you know baby, when you picked that puppy, I really wanted you to bring that puppy home but I couldn't deny Aadi."

"I was begging at that time," she said with anger, "but you made me leave him."

"Sorry baby, but even I am crazy about pets."

"Do you know, Neev, I have a dream."

"What dream, Aashi?"

"I want to build a kind of stable," she smiled.

"I don't understand. What 'kind of stable'?"

"I meant only horses live in stables otherwise, but in my stable there will be a place for every animal. Dogs, puppies, goats, cows, pigs; the one that has no owner to take care of them, I will provide them a shelter to live under, food to eat and water to drink. I will treat them with proper medicine.

"Do you know, Neev, whenever I see these animals, it makes me sad because they have no food, no water. And nobody who can take care of them. It's so pathetic that these animals can't say anything. That is why I want to take care of these animals."

I put one hand on her head as if in a blessing, "Great Aashi, you really have awesome thoughts and dreams. If I will be your husband, then I will definitely help you out to fulfil this dream."

She came closer to me and said, "If ever you leave me, I will be no more in this world, so never say this thing again. You definitely will be my husband, nobody else."

"Okay love, hope whatever you think will be fulfilled."

"You know, yesterday, the moment when you were crying for me thinking I am unconscious, I wanted to wake up just then. Soon, I realized I was feeling comfortable in your arms and I decided to live my whole life in your arms."

Just then, I looked at my watch it was around 9 p.m. I told Aashi about it.

She stood up and said, "I am going to bring dinner for you."

"Okay, love."

She left the room and I was thinking about Aashi's dream. I appreciated her dream. The admirable thing was that in today's times, there were still people who think for others, and not just humans. This dream of hers had brought me closer to Aashi.

Within a few minutes, she came again with the food. She came inside and placed the food on the table.

She was quiet; I was looking at her and suddenly spoke up, "Baby, if ever you leave me alone, I can't live without you even for a single day." I had tears in my eyes for her. She hugged me and kissed me on the lips. After that, she left the room saying jokingly, "Next time, don't cry like girls."

I had not eaten the food; I was thinking about Aashi. I was sitting near my window and was looking at her window. My heart was beating fast and wishing to see her at least once before going to sleep.

I somehow knew that Aashi would surely come. After a few minutes, she came with her paper and marker.

After seeing her, I stood and brought my things for communication. At that moment she was displaying "Eaten food or not?".

I replied, "No".

She asked, "Why?"

I wrote sympathetically, "Missing you, baby".

She wrote, "Oh darling, me too".

I was afraid of losing Aashi, because I did not have anyone else in my life to call my own. And right now, there was no favourable condition for me to marry her.

I wrote "good night" and left the window.

I was thinking about our future, the day when Aadi and his family would get to know about me.

The day will be unimaginable in more ways than I could imagine.

Next day, I was in Aashi's class. As usual, Aashi was sitting on the last bench. Whenever I had my eyes on her, she used to give out flying kisses, spread her arms for a hug and some such other things. None of the girl was noticing her, because now she was sitting alone on the last bench. I was not reacting to all this, but I wanted to dismiss the class and give her a hug.

The next thing, she wrote, "I love you" on the page and showed me. After seeing this, I couldn't stop myself and smiled. I was standing in between the class, teaching a topic, surrounded by many girls, and I began to laugh aloud.

I didn't have anything to say to justify this, so I said sorry to the class for interruption.

I thought I had managed to fool the girls, but at the last moment, Aashi stood up.

"Sir, this is not the right thing. You must share the joke with us also." I stopped laughing.

It was a typical situation for me to answer, as I had to maintain the decorum of class.

I did not look at Aashi and said I couldn't discuss that joke with the class.

Just five minutes were left for the class to get over; I left the class as soon as possible. After moving out from the class, I began to laugh out loudly once again. I was just remembering Aashi's activities in the class, telling myself how mad she was.

I had just entered the staff room when my eyes fell on Aadi and Aliya. They were sitting next to each other. I interrupted in between and asked if I was disturbing.

Aliya said, "No, it is okay. Come join us."

Aadi said, "Neev, how's your day going?"

"Yeah, it was fine. What about yours?" I smiled.

"Good, very good," Aadi replied looking at Aliya.

Aliya chuckled at his statement.

I could make out that Aadi had succeeded; it meant Aliya had accepted the proposal.

"Nowadays, it seems you have less work in office, Aadi?" I teased.

"No it isn't like that," he flushed, "I was just going."

He stood up and began leaving, but I ran towards him to talk personally.

"Saale, tell me what Aliya said. "

"Oye maan gayi yaar; she said yes, "Aadi sounded happy.

I was happy for Aadi because I knew he really loved her. I gave Aadi a tight hug and said, "Congrats, my dear." I was so excited and was talking in a loud voice.

She saw me; I was happy with their love.

"Okay, okay, relax! I need to go now," Aadi left me in the staff room with Aliya.

Aliya was sitting at the other end of the table; I just showed her thumbs up for best of luck. She slowly mumbled a thank you.

In the evening at 8, I was curiously waiting for Aashi. Today, we had many things to discuss. Even when we didn't have things to share, then also we loved to be with each other. Exactly at 8 p.m., I was desperately waiting for Aashi. The three knocks on the door made me happy; I was sure it was Aashi. I woke up from my bed and opened the door, but it was Aadi. He came inside and hugged me.

"I am very happy today, Neev. It's like a new life to me."

"So, where's the party?"

"Yeah of course, I am dying to celebrate. Let us go out for dinner."

"But Aadi, within minutes Aashi would be coming for her tuition."

"Don't worry, I told her earlier. She won't come."

I was thinking that I missed the chance to meet Aashi. I dressed up within minutes and moved for the party. I was getting down from the stairs and saw Aashi working in the kitchen. She saw me she turned her face to the other side. I knew I would hear many things from Aashi in our next session.

I had a great time with Aadi in a continental restaurant, but I missed Aashi.

It was 10 pm when we were entered the house. I was sure Aashi would have slept. My first duty after entering the house was to look at Aashi's window.

Exactly the opposite happened; she was still standing at the window.

I ran a bit faster for the room to get in touch with Aashi. I opened my door and picked the paper and marker. I opened my window and saw she was displaying something, "kill you soon".

I smiled after reading it and wrote, "Sorry, where is your mobile?"

"Still in the service centre," replied Aashi.

I wrote, "Okay, how is your hand, love?"

"Fine, I want to meet you in the restaurant tomorrow," she replied.

"Nope, I am sorry," I said.

"Then why did you go today"?

"Your brother is stubborn," I wrote.

"You know I am more stubborn than him and I have a headache," she said.

I was afraid of going out with her; if someone saw us, then it would be a big trouble for both.

I wrote, "good night and take some medicine" and closed the window. I used to keep all those papers safely in a file.

I had decided not to go outside with Aashi anyhow.

I was peeping out from a little hole in the window to know whether she had gone back in or not. When I saw, she was still displaying some text. It was difficult to see what was written. However, after changing many angles, without opening the window I read that – "Will not move, till you agree."

Oh my god, she is a true stubborn. I opened the window and wrote, "Okay, we will think tomorrow".

"No thinking, I want to go."

"Okay honey," I told her.

I decided that we would go out in the evening itself, so that we can be home in good time. I was thinking of Aashi's headache. She had been complaining of it often but still didn't take it seriously. I was worried if it was something serious or could cause more problems with her in future. She never discussed these spasms of pain with her parents. Whenever I used to ask her to have any good treatment for this pain, she always avoided me by saying, "I hate doctors".

Next day, I was continuing the previous day's leftover topic in Aashi's class. Suddenly a girl stood up and asked how to prepare for the university exam.

They had fourth semester exams at the end of the month. I guided her to start preparing from the sample papers and previous year exam papers, as in accounts the examination pattern was mostly the same.

I looked at Aashi; she had picked her notebook facing towards me and something was written on it. While pretending to discuss the topic in detail, I went near the last bench where she was sitting, so that none of the girls could understand that there was something fishy.

"MC DONALD'S,

A-46 M.G. ROAD, AGRA.

AT 5:00 P.M".

Oh my god, I had never thought she would be capable of doing something like this. I had no other option except agreeing with her.

Somehow, I managed to complete the day. I was waiting for Aashi in my room for lunch.

Someone knocked at the door and I opened it; Aashi was standing in front of me.

She put the food on the table and came closer to me. First, she hugged me. I came down in a calm manner and said, "Baby, try to understand if in case we're seen by someone, then it will be a great trouble for both. Please try to understand."

I already knew she had no regard for my convincing her, but still I tried.

"It was already decided. You just have to take a direct auto from Kar Kunj Chouraha to Mc Donald's; it will take you about twenty-five minutes to reach," she chirped.

"So you will not stop?" I chided her.

"No baby. Now, come on, come on and give me a kiss."

I smiled and kissed on her forehead.

"And also tell me what I should say to your brother about where I am going," I asked her because that's what I had been thinking the whole morning.

She pulled herself back and said, "Are you a kid that you need to take permission from someone else? Just tell him you have to go to the market to buy some books or accessories."

"Okay, madam, and what will you say at home? You are the kid of the house and you will have to tell them where you're going."

"I will manage all that; don't worry for me." I was surprised at her confidence but still did not give up on convincing her.

"Please Aashi, try to get my point, love. I know we would have fun together there. Moreover, it is very risky to meet you outside now; many people know me. If in case someone sees us, do you even realise what would be the end result?"

I had tried all my ways to convince Aashi and finally she understood me.

"Okay, if you are insisting so much then we are not going to meet. I can't see you so worried. But no one can stop me from loving you, my darling." She smiled her charismatic smile and I gave her a quick peck.

The peck turned into a long drawn kiss and she left my room after a while.

It's quite true that there are ups and downs in love. Such things make one upset, but after that the love train will continue to run on the track, without any care of the world. Aashi and Neev were travelling in this train, and they didn't want to stop, no matter what.

One reason why I was so attached to Aashi was that she was a kind-hearted girl as compared to other girls of her age. She was transparent; nothing could be hidden inside her. A girl like Aashi can make everyone love her.

Her heart was so beautiful. As I sat on my bed thinking about this wonderful girl, her face was before my eyes. Now, there was only one question in my mind – Will Aashi be my better half or not?

7

PHOTO SHOOT

Only a month remained for Aashi's university exams. As usual, she came to my room and started her jolly activities, but I realised her studies were taking a back seat. I wanted to know how much she was ready for the exams. Without warning, I asked Aashi how much syllabus she had covered for her exams. Aashi was an average student; she always got average marks in exams. So even though there was no need to ask such questions, I asked about her preparation for my satisfaction.

She hesitated, but finally came up with the truth, "Neev, frankly speaking I am completely nil in this semester; I have not prepared a single subject this time."

"And in my subject? Did you get something there?"

"Nope."

"Oh, my god! Are you nuts? What would you do in your exams?"

"I don't know baby, and I don't want to think about

it also. Please don't give goose bumps to me; change the topic."

"Shut up, I want you to score good marks, Aashi."

"I will try my best in exams, Neev. Please don't be angry."

"What will you do in exams if you don't study now? Not in exams, from now onwards…"

I opened her notebook and made a timetable for her.

"What is this?" she asked me innocently, as if not understanding what I was up to.

"Can't you see, this is your new timetable for studies? No more gossips and flirting, just studying when you are in my room. Am I clear?"

She nodded and asked me excitedly, "Will you teach me all the subjects?"

"Yes, till you are well prepared for all your exams. I will manage all that."

She left the room as the tuition time was over. She was always punctual, so that no one in the family can think of anything else.

I had made two copies of that timetable; one copy for Aashi and the other for myself.

Next day in college, after my lectures, I went to the library to study the subjects that I had to teach Aashi according to the timetable. I was amused to think that I had never prepared my subjects like this while I was doing my graduation.

There was also a day when I was studying in the library and suddenly Aadi came to inquire about the budget of new books from the librarian. He saw me and said with a wink, "Teachers have become students now! Who's making you study all over again?"

"Oh, I am just preparing for my next lecture," I lied to him.

He took a seat next to mine. I knew he wasn't convinced with my reason. So I tried diverting his mind.

"Hey Aadi, do you remember the warden of our hostel?"

He narrowed his eyes slightly, "Of course, I do".

"During college, he was always in your favour, and took your side in most matters. He is a really nice friend of yours, I guess."

"Fuck off, man! He was not a nice guy; I made him nice," he boasted. Aadi was caught in my word-web owing to his inclination to brag.

"What do you mean, Aadi?"

He said animatedly, "Yes, really! He always created trouble for me in the beginning. Whenever we used to have non-veg food inside the hostel, he had a problem; whenever we bought wine and beer, he complained to the Dean."

I encouraged him, "Oh, yes! I do remember. You were even rusticated from the college for a week when you were caught with the beer cans in the room."

"That is what I was telling you; I changed him."

"What did you do to him to change him? Share with me also, yaar."

He just pulled his chair closer to mine and began whispering his story.

"When I was rusticated from the college, it hurt me a lot. The entire one week after that, I did only one thing – planning."

"Planning? What planning?"

"I will tell you," he said, and continued, "I had decided to give a feedback to the warden for his dirty activities. In those days, I used to have contacts with the people living in the nearby area. Some of them dealt with girls. Somehow, some of the people were on good terms with me. I discussed my problem with them. They suggested me something and excitedly, I also decided to perform the task.

"The warden was around twenty-five years old at that time; he was newly married and due to college rules and regulations, he couldn't complete his honeymoon. His hometown was a good four hundred kilometres from college.

"One day, he was wandering in the market area and suddenly a beautiful lady got in touch with him. She asked the way to our college. Then he asked the lady what work she had in college.

She told him that she had come for an interview for B.Com. he informed her that the interview timing has been long over. At that, the lady started panicking that she had especially come from

Firozabad for the interview and could not even go back in the evening to come back again the next day. He promised that he will try to help, being the warden of the college. He took that lady on his old scooter, which had "Hamara Bajaj" written at the back in bold.

"He asked her name; she told him it was Sheetal. He said, 'Nice name. Now, I am going to take you to a hotel near our college. It will have nominal charges with all facilities available. You can stay there for the night and tomorrow if you are selected, then I will arrange for you within the hostel itself.'

"She said thank you to him and told him how kind he was. I had reached the hotel with my Canon digital camera before them. And I was already aware that he would definitely take that girl to the same hotel because that's where all the college guests stayed. The warden went with her to show her the room. They entered one of the rooms; the hotel was not so good. I had told Sheetal to flirt with the warden.

"In the meantime, I reached the window at the back of the room. Sheetal saw the room, came closer to him and gave him a hug, and kept insisting how good a person he was. As she made him busy, I clicked a few pictures.

"He requested her to not go any closer and got up to leave the room. I knew that he was a decent and well-mannered person. He didn't want to make use of the available condition, but Sheetal wanted to earn money. I had promised her five hundred bucks.

"Surprisingly, she caught hold of his hand in hers and pulled him towards her. She kissed him hard on the lips and he lost all his control.

I was happy to see them as I was getting a great view to click all the pictures of them. I loved the technology of clicking photos without a flash, thanks Canon.

"In the next fifteen minutes, I had created an entire album. After the work was over, Sheetal gave her introduction and mine as well. She left the room without waiting for any college interview. When the warden heard my name from Sheetal, he was completely shocked and puzzled. He didn't waste a single moment in the room and reached my room.

"I heard a knock on my door as if someone was striking it with a hammer. I had a very sweet smile on my face as I looked at the photographs, but I left my work and opened the door. He came inside to the room and asked me why I had done all that. I acted innocent, but soon his eyes fell on the pictures. He was furious. He threatened to kill me; and was also willing to complain to the dean; he was obviously scared of losing his job as well.

"I told him, 'Go on, sir! You can complain to the Dean while I freshen up. Then I will go and post these photos to your home town. Your wife will be glad to see you in these pictures. See, how clear these pictures are! And Sheetal is also looking so very gorgeous.'

"He understood that he was in trouble now, and asked me what I wanted from him. I frankly told him that I just wanted him to shut his mouth till I was a student in the college and allow me to do what I wished to. I also promised that he would get the pictures back the day I passed out of college and nobody will ever get to know of them"

I was sniggering by now; Aadi had been a clever boy and had set the warden up real good.

Aadi continued, "The warden pleased that stopping me was his mistake, and so was his time with Sheetal. I was relentless. I told him, 'Whatever that may be, I want you to make such mistakes daily, till the time I am in this hostel.'

"I laughed and asked him if he agreed to my condition. He knew he was not left with an option other than accepting this one. So he put his hand on the head and left the room. And from that day onward, he automatically began talking and acting in my favour. After this incident, I used to bring wine, whisky, beer, chicken, mutton and all such stuff into the room and he never uttered a word." Aadi concluded his story with great pride.

I was impressed, really. I told him, "Oh my god, Aadi. How many secrets are still buried in your heart? You didn't discuss these things with us while we were in college."

"Nothing like that yaar, it's just that I had promised the warden that none other than me will get to know about this."

I said sarcastically, "Oh, yes! How can I forget what a true person you are, Aadi. Once a commitment made to someone, is like words carved in stone."

Both of us chuckled, and Aadi suddenly spoke up, "Hey Neev! I forgot to tell you that today I had talked to mom and dad about Aliya. They were slightly puzzled and reluctant after hearing that she belongs to some other caste to begin with, but they agreed for Aliya at the end."

I was happy for him. "Oh, my god, Aadi. That's great news, and you are telling me this so late. Congratulations, yaar! I got up from the chair and gave him a hug.

"Have you guys fixed up a date yet?" I was curious.

Aliya had told me that she can marry only after six months. And I agreed readily because I also love winters.

"Good, that will be a great time. Hey, I need to discuss one more thing with you," I told him.

"Yeah Neev, tell me what happened?"

"Yaar Aadi, I am planning to buy a plot here. I have managed to save that much money from my salary."

Aadi looked happy at my proposition; I knew he had always been my well-wisher. "Good idea, Neev! It's a great thought. I will talk to one of my friends who deals in buying and selling of plots and let you know."

"Thanks, brother. And one more thing, if you like that plot, give him the advance. I will pay you."

He nodded and we left the library together, as by now, other people were getting disturbed and staring at the two of us whispering away to glory. I went down to the staff room and towards Aliya to congratulate her.

I was planning to buy that plot to fulfil Aashi's dream and wanted to give her a surprise. For a month, I had worked hard to save that money. Only for Aashi.

On the eve of the last day of her exams, Aashi was sitting right next to me in my room and she suddenly hugged me.

"What happened, baby?" I was concerned.

"Neev, tomorrow is my last exam and then I will not able to come for tuitions. There will be summer vacation for one month, so we won't be able to meet each other in college also. We will get no such chances to spend time together," she said with tears in her eyes.

I told her, "Why are you worrying? We will talk through phone and please concentrate on your studies till tomorrow. Don't think of all this now."

She continued studying, but still had tears in her eyes.

I was worried for her exams, though.

Next day in the evening, she send me a text message, "I love you".

I replied, "I love you too baby, how was your exam?"

She replied, "It was good. I have a plan".

I suddenly became very anxious to hear that word from her mouth. Still, I gathered some guts and called her up to ask, "What plan are you talking about, Aashi?"

"Okay, Neev. In the beginning itself I am saying, I am just discussing the plan, and not asking you whether we should do it or not."

"Yeah, as usual. There's nothing new about it," I chuckled.

"Stop it, and listen to what I am saying. I have a cousin named Nisha Sharma. She is an engineer and working in Bangalore in an MNC."

"That's good. So what we can do for her?"

"Let me finish, at least. Where was I?... Yes, Nisha and I are very close. We are very good friends also and share all our things. And guess what, today I have discussed you with her."

I was happy that Aashi was confident enough about me to have shared it with someone so close to her, but the next moment was clouded with doubt, "Aashi, if she tells Aadi, then it will be trouble for us."

"Don't worry, mister worried. She is my pal, always on my side. I have faith on her. So come to the point, I have decided that you should meet her."

"Okay, so when is she coming?"

"She is not coming; we are going to Bangalore."

"Are you crazy? I am not going to Bangalore. It's just too far from Agra for comforts."

"Am I asking you to travel to Bangalore by foot? It takes only four hours from Delhi by plane. And I know you are not a miser."

I was stunned as to how she came up with such stuff all the time, "Oh my god, Aashi. I don't know anyone in Bangalore."

"Do you want to start a business there?"

"Okay, I got the point. Now tell me this also. What will I tell Aadi? And will your parents allow you to go to Bangalore?"

"Just tell him that you are going to spend some time at Dadri, your hometown on vacation and I have talked to dad already. He is going with me and he will stay there for some three-four days. After that, he will come back. And you should reach Bangalore once dad gets back here.

The very next day, Aashi and her dad left for Bangalore. Their flight was from Delhi airport. Aashi was in constant touch with me.

I told Aadi about my plan of spending a few days in Dadri. After three days, Aashi texted me, "Dad has left for Agra. Book your ticket for tomorrow".

At the same time, I booked my ticket for Bangalore without telling Aadi. I had packed my luggage and was ready to move. Firstly, I had to take a bus for Delhi and from Delhi airport, I would get my flight.

I was sitting and waiting at the Agra bus stand; it was vacation time, so many people were going to their destination. My bus would move after an hour, so unwillingly I had to wait at the bus stand.

Right opposite me sat a couple with their luggage. They seemed newly-wed. Suddenly the boy came near me, making me think he had come to complain that I was staring at his wife. But thankfully, he only asked me to click their photograph.

He called his wife to stand next to him. I clicked their picture; the girl thanked me and said, "We want to capture every moment of our honeymoon, to refresh our love every day".

"Wow, that's really so sweet. Wish you a happy journey," I said.

I saw an image of Aashi in that women. I was missing her a lot.

I was very excited to spend time with Aashi. I had made a lot of plans. But truly speaking, I was scared. I have a fear of this world, the people who are selfish and cruel. In reality, people are not as we see in movies. It's a completely different world.

And this was going to be my first time with a girl. It's a very big responsibility to take care of her in a new city.

I was lost in thought when my bus came in. I took my seat in the bus; it was going to be a four-hour journey to Delhi.

I got my flight on time and within I had texted Aashi before boarding the flight that I would be in Bangalore by the same evening.

August 2011

I was standing outside the airport and the weather was awesome. It felt as if I was visiting a hill station. Bangalore gets heavy rain during monsoon. According to people of the city, the monsoon changes three times in autumn itself.

I fell in love with Bangalore at the first sight.

I picked up my phone and rang Aashi to ask what was to be done next.

"Hey baby, I am standing in Bangalore."

She almost squeeked with happiness, "Oh, my love. So sweet of you. Thanks for coming, baby."

I was glad that I could make her so happy. "My pleasure dear. Tell me what to do next?"

She said excitedly, "I am sending you a text having my cousin's address; take a taxi for that place. It should not cost more than a hundred bucks."

"One minute, I am not going to stay at your cousin's house. Give me the address of some good hotel. I will stay there and we will meet during the day," I clarified my intentions.

She didn't seem to have liked the idea much, "Are you mad? Neev, there is no formality here. She does not have a problem with your living in her flat. Do you understand?"

"Nope, I am sorry but I feel shy. I don't want to give her any trouble."

"Oh my god, you are a fool. I don't know any hotel here, so come to this address straight and don't create unnecessary fuss for all of us. Why can you not listen to me in the first go?"

Her anger was rising, but I would never have done what was not right. "Okay, I will arrange a hotel for myself and will talk to you once I am settled."

She shouted, "Go to hell" and disconnected the phone. She felt that I was being formal; but more than that, I would have felt very odd at someone else's house.

I was standing at the terminal and waiting for the taxi. I asked one cabbie to take me to some 3 star hotel, so that I can manage in the city within my stipulated budget.

First, I tried to explain what I wished to say in Hindi as it's my mother tongue. I got puzzled and excitedly, he said, "I know Kannada and English".

I was shocked that a taxi driver knows English. Then I remembered that this was not Agra; this was Bangalore.

The taxi driver dropped me at an average hotel near the bus terminus. It was the most positive thing for me, because the location made it easy for me to inquire about the tourist places from there.

After settling down my luggage in my room, I called up Aashi to let her know my exact address. Nisha picked up my phone instead as Aashi was in the bathroom.

The first question she asked in her soft voice was, "Where are you staying?"

I gave her my complete address and she told it was very near to her flat. She also told me that she and Aashi would come over to my room by the time I freshen up, and I gave her my room number. I was puzzled after hearing this, and was excited also.

I gave her the complete address and they reached within thirty minutes.

I was excited to meet them, more so to meet Aashi. I opened the door and suddenly Aashi jumped on me. She hugged me and kissed my forehead ever so lightly.

She cooed, "Baby, I missed you so much. Why don't you come home?"

"I also missed you immensely, baby. It's been three days. But I am comfortable here. I don't want to disturb you both.

"Alright, even I am standing here," came a low soft voice. It was Nisha.

"Sorry, Nisha. Please come in, dear."

She was looking beautiful. I gave her a hug and asked her how she had been doing.

She replied just as politely, "Good! But I am angry with you."

"Angry with me? But why?"

"You should have stayed in my house; that's your own yaar," she complained.

"Sorry for that, Nisha, but I would have felt very awkward. Hope you understand."

She smiled, nodded and continued, "You know how much Aashi was missing you. Every moment, she had only one name and that was Neev. I was really curious to meet the person who had stolen my sister's heart."

Aashi was still holding my hand and said excitedly, "So Nisha? Isn't he too goo?"

We all started laughing loudly after the statement.

I ordered the food for all three of us. Nisha told me to get back to her flat.

I ignored her and asked her to set our programme for the tour and was told that Aashi had fixed the whole programme already.

"I am impressed, Aashi." Looking at Nisha, I asked, "You will be joining us, right?"

"No, actually I have some important project going on. So it's difficult for me to join you and I am really very upset for this," Nisha said.

"Don't worry, Nisha, we can wait for you," I said in a humble manner.

"Oh that is so sweet, Neev, but please ask your love if she would allow you to wait for some more time."

"No, no, no. I can't wait anymore. I am dying to see Goa."

I gave Aashi a puzzled look and said, "You are so excited that you are calling Bangalore Goa." But she continued to smile, and knowing what all she was capable of, I asked her, "Aashi, are we going to Goa?"

"Yes, my love. We are going to Goa."

"Oh, my god. You are really mad. So how far is Goa from here?"

"It's around one night by bus and Neev, you can't imagine how much fun we will have there."

We had the supper and I asked both to stay in the room.

But Aashi denied and said she had to pack her entire luggage the same night itself as the next evening, she had already booked tickets for Goa.

I was slightly disappointed, "So Aashi, we are not going to see Bangalore?"

"There is nothing special to see in Bangalore," she justified.

Aashi was dying to see Goa; it could be easily noticed from her face. And I can do anything to see this charm on her face.

Nisha stood up and said, "Let's go Aashi, one of my friends is coming home".

Nisha was standing at the door and Aashi mumbled in my ear, "Baby, take care of yourself and lock the door when we leave the room. If you face any kind of problem, just call me, okay?"

I laughed, "Aashi, I am not a child and don't you think you are saying my dialogues?"

I gave her a kiss on the forehead and asked her to leave as Nisha was waiting.

They both left the room and got back to their flat.

As Aashi reached the flat, she texted me. I called her up.

"Aashi, I am missing you."

"Oh baby, I too am dying to spend time with you."

"I want to see you, love."

"That will be possible tomorrow only; it's pretty late now."

"But Aashi, I want see you now. Just text me the address and tell me where is Nisha?"

"She had some urgent work; she dropped me and left for office."

While the conversation was on, Aashi had texted me the address. After receiving the text I locked the door and left for the flat.

I asked Aashi how many days we were going to spend in Goa and the same moment, I also managed to hop into a taxi for Nisha's flat. I had worked in a way so that Aashi didn't come to know I was on my way already. I had not discussed that I was sitting in the taxi. Within twenty minutes, I reached the door and told Aashi that I could give her a surprise.

"What surprise?" she asked me excitedly.

Count till three and you will have the surprise.

She started counting aloud – "1...2...3..." and just then, I knocked on the door.

She told me over phone, "Neev, I guess someone has come. Let me see first, you hold the line." She opened the door and I shouted, "Surprise, baby".

She just ran into my arms and kissed me on the lips, shouting, "Oh my baby, I love you, I love you. Why didn't you tell me you were coming?"

"Then how would I give you a surprise?" I smiled at her happiness.

We slept after talking for a while; she had put her head on my shoulder.

She said, "What was the need to come now when you kept refusing to begin with?"

She was right but I told her the real reason, "I was missing you, love."

"So? We were going to meet tomorrow anyway," she teased.

"Very good. When you missed me, you called me from Agra to Bangalore. And I don't have a right to meet you within the city also? So unfair."

"We spent a few more minutes together and I left for my hotel as I didn't want Nisha to know of my visit.

There are lots of things which I dislike about Aashi, and there are many things which she hates about me. But there is one common thread which connects both of us – our love for each other. We were crazy for each other. We have only one option to express, and that is to make love. And we are perfect for each other in expressing this. The way she hugs me, the way she kisses me, the way she goes crazy at any time for loving me, to see me. All these things were enough for me to love her. I knew I couldn't live without her. So I never thought of our differences. I accept everything she wants and by seeing all this, she falls in love with me every moment. Sometimes I crossed my fingers with a fear that Aashi might leave me one day, but I had faith in my love. It was also true that I had broken Aadi's and his family's faith in me; I knew I will hurt them one day.

But when I saw Aashi, everything felt alright. Our love was enough for us and I was going to love her forever.

The world of love is full of light where we don't want to imagine darkness. Better to say we can't see worse behind the charm of love. Can't say love makes us blind or we are blind in love, both are equal. Love chokes all senses. Love makes people immature. It was exactly what happened with Aashi and Neev, and they had no idea.

8

NIGHTS IN GOA

Love is an amazing feeling, when lovebirds fly, nothing can stop them. They find out their way. They reach a point, where all senses stop working. They can't then differentiate between wrong and right. They follow just one rule – everything is fair in love. Little do these lovebirds know that love gives pain also. When two innocent hearts fall in love, they don't know that they will cry when they face this world, which doesn't understand the language of love.

Aashi and I sat waiting for the bus that would take us to Goa. The bus stand named "VIJAYNANDA TRAVELS" was a private bus stand, the only place from where you can get bus for any place in south India. After a few moments, Aashi and I took our seats inside the bus while Nisha stood outside. She had come to drop Aashi and I had reached on my own.

Nisha smiled and asked Aashi, "So lovers, what have you planned about coming back?

Aashi shouted, "Never Nisha janu."

Nisha said in mock horror, "Don't say this otherwise your mom and dad will kill me."

"Don't worry Nisha, we will be back soon. We have not planned a very long trip."

"Okay Neev, I trust you and that's why I am allowing Aashi to go."

"Oh, it means I am a fool," shouted Aashi and broke into laughter.

As the bus started moving, Aashi put a blanket on both of us. The seat booked was air-conditioned semi sleeper. The bus in charge had already issued the blankets. Inside the blanket, Aashi picked up my hand and put it on her heart.

Aashi said, "Neev baby, I love you. Never leave me alone."

"Never baby, not until my last breath."

She put her head on my shoulder and mumbled, "Baby, I need this shoulder to support me till my last breath. Will you?"

"Aashi, why are you getting so emotional?"

"Neev, I am missing my family."

I caressed her forehead and said, "Aww, darling, am I not included in your family?"

"Yes Neev, you are my family. I had broken their faith and trust only for you."

I consoled her, "Aashi, don't get upset. Just enjoy these moments."

At around 8:00 p.m. Aashi switched off the light of our seat. She had come closer to me; my heart was beating fast after seeing her trust and faith on me. I was worried if I would be able to fulfil all responsibilities towards Aashi in future.

I picked up her hand and took her head in my lap, so that she could sleep more comfortably.

She had closed her eyes, as she was tired. I was seeing her face in the moon light as all the artificial lights were switched off in the bus. She was looking like an angel. It was sure that she was a gift for me by god. As I had nothing left in my life after dad, Aashi had come in my life and made me cherish every moment. She nourished me with her love. While I was thinking all this, I was missing my dad. I was thinking if my family was there, then they would do all formalities for me to get married with Aashi. My eyes were filled with tears. I knew she belonged to a higher caste than mine. I was worried whether her parents will accept me or not. And I have no guts to stand in front of them and fight against them, as they have done a lot for me. I didn't realise but my tears were falling down; Aashi opened her eyes after a few tears fell on her face.

"What happened, Neev?"

"Nothing dear, why did you wake up?"

"Why are you crying?"

"I was just thinking of our future, whether your parents will allow me to get married to you or not."

"Oh baby, don't think about all that." She wiped my tears with her soft hands and said, "You only had told me to enjoy these moments and now you are crying. This is not good."

"Aashi, I love you. I can't live without you. I am worried whether we can get married or not," I could not hold back any longer.

"Of course Neev, we will get married. Don't you worry," she consoled me. We were sitting on the last seat of the bus, so there was no one to interrupt us.

We were so emotionally close to each other, that we couldn't stop ourselves and were smooching in the bus itself. I wanted to make more love to her, but we followed the rules of transport and slept.

It was morning 10:00 a.m., and we were about to reach Goa. Aashi was still sleeping; I woke her up as we were about to reach our destination.

She woke up lazily and combed her hair.

I was slightly worried because we had not made any bookings for us. The first thing would be to search for an accommodation.

The bus dropped us at the Panjim bus stand in Goa. We were standing and just watching our surroundings. I was confused.

Suddenly, two bikers came near us and asked us if we needed any help.

I told them to suggest any of the hotels nearby. They suggested we move to Panjim City. Since we did not have any other mode of transport, they asked for fifty bucks for each bike and they would drop us to the hotel. I agreed because I had no other option.

Both of us sat on different bikes and within ten minutes, they dropped us there. That's when I came to know that in

Goa, at some places, bikes are used as taxis as well.

Unwillingly, I had paid a hundred bucks for such a short distance. It was clear that they cheated us, but it didn't matter, because they dropped us to the correct destination.

We were standing in front of the hotel named "Joseph villa". It was looking good and I was worried about its rent. Aashi went to inquire. The rent was not that much, so we agreed to stay there.

We were given a good enough room. It was 3:00 p.m. and we were hungry. So first we got fresh, and then ordered lunch from the hotel kitchen itself.

Aashi was waiting for food; she had washed her hair and was looking very cute. In the meantime we were discussing the places to visit. We had planned to rest that day and the next day had the final programme of going to the casino. Aashi was dying to see the beach. Mostly girls love beaches and Aashi was one of them. We had planned to see the beach day after the next.

The waiter got our food, both of us ate the food and were watching television.

I kept changing the channels, as I was not finding the perfect channel. Aashi was watching me angrily and suddenly she sat on my stomach and asked me not to change the channel. She was looking cool in that pose; she came closer to my face and kissed on my forehead. I put her down and kissed on her lips. She was not feeling comfortable while sitting on my stomach; she got down and slept next to me.

My hand was on her stomach and she had closed her eyes. I mumbled slowly in her ears, "I love you, baby".

She replied, "Make love to me, Neev".

My heart was beating fast; I put my hand on her cheeks and started kissing her.

Suddenly Aashi moved to the other corner of the bed and asked me to do the same. I was anxious to see what she had in mind.

She took off her pyjama. She was sitting nude in front of me. I left everything and got closer to her. I put my hands on her and closed my eyes to lock that feeling in my heart forever. The aroma of her body was unforgettable.

We slept in each other's arms and I was the first one to wake up around 11:00 p.m., that too with a feeling that something was biting me. I didn't want to wake up Aashi because both of us were tired after the long journey. Again, I managed to sleep but I was feeling that something was crawling on my chest. I was scared of insects; I switched on my mobile light and looked at the bed.

There were a lot of bedbugs on the blanket and bed. I ran from my bed and switched on the light to look at them clearly.

I didn't wake up Aashi, as I didn't want to disturb her. I was sitting on the bed and picked a water glass to collect all the bedbugs, so that they don't bite Aashi.

I was searching for bedbug on Aashi's side without disturbing her, so that none of them could bite her. I was concentrating at every corner of Aashi's side, so none of them could touch my baby; I left the bed and planned to wake up the whole night.

I did this for almost two hours and finally I could collect all the bedbugs, not a single bedbug was there on the bed. I didn't sleep for the whole night.

I was awake; Aashi looked adorable in her sleep; I kept looking at her with love; how could I sleep? I took my diary out and went into the hotel lobby, lest she wakes up with the light.

I was penning down my diary around and it was around 1:00 a.m. After finishing, I got back on my duty of searching bedbugs. I was searching them with the help of my mobile's backlight.

It was 3:00 a.m. and still I was finding bedbugs. I didn't know from where they all were coming, but I didn't care about them coming. My purpose was to rid the bed of them.

In looking for those insects, I reached Aashi's thighs. Suddenly, Aashi woke up and sensing something happening around her legs, she shouted, "Who are you? Wake up, Neev! See who's this man here."

I put my mobile's backlight on my face and said, "Baby, it's me, Neev. Don't worry."

"Neev, what you were doing?"

She switched on the light.

"Aashi, on our bed there are many bedbugs and I was catching them, so that they do not bite you."

"Oh my god, since when you have you been doing this?"

"From 11:00 p.m.," I answered.

"Are you nuts? Why didn't you wake me up?"

"You were so tired that I didn't feel like waking you up."

"Oh baby, come on, hug me sweetheart."

At last I got my reward of collecting bedbugs.

She chuckled and called at the reception, so that he could get the blankets changed.

Within a few minutes, the staff had come with the new blankets. As he came inside the room Aashi shouted, "Is this the 'service' you provide to your guests? Do you know because of your mistake, our whole night has been wasted."

He said apologetically, "Sorry madam, it's due to the rainy season."

"So you mean to say that if there are rains, then you will allow us to sleep with the bedbugs?" Aashi was taking his case.

After hearing Aashi's voice, the manager of the hotel came inside and apologised. He fired the attendant who had been 'arguing' with the 'guest'. Though the manager left after that, Aashi kept feeling guilty that because of her the waiter had to leave the job.

I asked her not to worry and that I will speak to the manager the next morning.

Next day, we woke up late and asked the manager about the adventurous things to do. He told us that in this season, all the adventurous sports are off. Due to rains, the waves are high so the adventure sports are all shut down. Though the beaches are open and can be enjoyed more fully.

"Okay what else is there to have fun in Goa?" I asked.

"Okay what else is there to have fun in Goa?" I asked.

He advised us to go to the Casino. Aashi seemed pretty excited at the thought of going to the casino; so I booked two tickets. The tickets were expensive, around three thousand bucks each. But I managed to buy them. We had to leave at 9:00 p.m. In the day, Aashi was dying to go to the beach. I promised to take her to the beach the next day.

We were passing our time roaming at the Panjim local bazaar in the evening. It was famous for fish.

Aashi asked me, "Neev, are you a vegetarian or a non-vegetarian?"

I told her that I was a non-vegetarian till I came in to their house.

"Okay, did you ever drink?"

"No, I don't drink. And I never have."

"Neev, you know, I want to try non-veg food and with it, unlimited wine. The day I get that chance, I don't want to count the glasses also. I just want to drink as much as I can.

"You have weird wishes, you know. But I like the first one of making a shelter for homeless animals."

She looked at me, her eyes reflecting immense love, "Aww baby, you still remember that?"

"How can I forget that honey? It's my dream also now," I held her close to me.

"Do you promise to help me fulfil that dream?"

"I promise, baby," I hugged her.

We were sitting on one shore of the Mandovi river, famous for its 'Goa by night' cruises in small boats with Goan music and dance. We were waiting for the casino to open. Exactly at 9:00 p.m. the gates opened. The staff of the casino gave us a warm welcome; I was glad because we had paid them a lot of money. They arranged for a motor boat to drop us to the casino. It was built in the middle of the river, afloat on the beautiful waters. We were excited to see that, as for both it was the first time. Aashi had held my hand and was kissing on my cheeks repeatedly, as she was happy to see all that. We reached the casino and the staff guided us in. There were two sections in the casino – one for playing and the other for unlimited food and drinks.

I mumbled to Aashi, "Today, you can fulfil your second dream."

She smiled and said, "I definitely will."

First, we moved to the gaming section. I was unaware of every game. I asked Aashi if she wanted to try her hand at any. She asked me to buy coins worth five hundred bucks. I bought those coins from the counter and gave them to Aashi. While taking the coins from me, she mumbled, "Just wait and watch how much I will earn with this."

I laughed, knowing full well that she wouldn't be able to do too much with those coins."

She came to the first counter and the game was called "black". I was unaware of the game per se but within moments, she earned two thousand bucks with it.

I was shocked on seeing her, and asked her where she had learnt this from. She answered, "Nisha".

We were happy as well as excited too and I told Aashi to get back, as I was afraid that she might lose the next game. She even joked that she can earn back the amount I had spent on the tickets but I asked her to let it be.

So we moved to the other section that provided the food and drinks.

I was seeing Aashi; she was getting excited to gorge on non-veg food and drink for the first time. I was mumbling, *"Aaj nahi bachega ye* casino*"*.

Aashi was smiling. We took the table and sat. As the waiter saw us, he came near us and asked about the order.

Aashi excitedly interrupted the waiter and said, "What are the things on the non-veg menu?"

He replied with a long list of items, which included crabs, fish, mutton, chicken and everything one could think of.

She said without thinking even once, "Bring one portion of each, please."

The waiter was taken aback at first, but as it was his duty, he noted down the order.

I won't say I wasn't shocked myself. I asked her how she would eat all that. But she just gave her characteristic smile and asked me, "Why? Are you fasting, Neev?"

"No, I am not. But…"

"So? You will help me."

I merely nodded with a smile.

Within ten minutes, five plates of non-veg food were placed on the table.

Aashi shouted, "Excuse me. Don't you have manners of serving? The food is not placed without drinks.

The Waiter saw Aashi was bragging a lot, he suddenly said, "I am sorry madam, what would you like to have?"

Aashi did not know anything about drinks, so she looked at me expectantly.

I asked the waiter to bring two pegs of "Signature".

Within a minute, he offered the remaining things, Aashi was excited to eat.

She was asking about every bite of the food. It feels that she is going to write the recipe list after going from there. She asked me how to drink, as my college experience of living with great friends was working now.

I taught her to drink slowly, by tasting food after every sip of drink.

She had drunk the whole glass and ordered one more glass. I told her to drink in limit, otherwise she might vomit. It was, after all, her first time.

But she didn't listen to me; she was enjoying the fulfilment of her dream. She was competing with me in the ratio 2:1. I had drunk five glasses and her count had reached ten.

She was moving on the chair, couldn't even sit properly.

Suddenly she shouted, "Waiter, come here!"

The same person came, "Yes madam".

"What is your name?"

"Madam, my name is Anthony."

"Anthony, are you the same who worked in the movie *Amar Akbar Anthony*?"

"No, Madam."

I stood up to stop Aashi, but I also was tipsy. I tried to convince her to sit down and asked Anthony to go.

The waiter had started moving when suddenly Aashi shouted again, "Excuse me, all guests and the staff of this casino. I want to make an announcement."

Every single person had started paying attention towards her.

I made Aashi sit in the chair, but Aashi didn't stop and continued her speech,

"I want to give the best waiter award in the whole world to Mr. Anthony from *Amar Akbar Anthony*. Sorry, I forgot that he had not worked in that movie."

I put my hand on my head; I didn't know what to do. She was completely out of control. Suddenly the manager came near me and said, "Please sir, madam is disturbing our customers. Could you please take her out?"

"Yeah, definitely," I said apologetically. I looked at Aashi at that time; she was picking up the bones of chicken and tucking them in the waiters' pockets.

I was thankful that nobody said a thing to her. And somehow, I managed to move out of there.

It was 1:00 a.m. by the time we came out; I was shivering due to the effects of liquor. Our hotel was not more than fifteen minutes' walk away. I held Aashi's hand. We were about to reach our hotel and suddenly Aashi saw a tree. She stopped at the same moment and asked me, "Do you love me, Neev?"

"Yeah, of course Aashi. We would talk about this in the room. Let's go!"

"Nope, we will talk right now. Tell me, do you love me?"

"Yes dear, I love you."

"Does it mean you can do anything for me?"

"Yes, definitely. Don't you feel we should talk about this topic in our room Aashi?" I just wanted to make her move from the road.

"No, Neev. If you love me, just climb this tree." She made a puppy face and looked very cute, but I was dead tired to do any such thing and told her the same.

"I don't know anything. If you love me, then climb up the tree right now or just leave my hand."

I knew she won't budge till I do what she was saying. As I moved closer to the tree, she ran towards me and hugged me from the back, "I was joking, baby. Let's go!"

I felt slightly relaxed, thanking god it was a joke.

I made her move towards the room with great difficulty.

A security guard was sitting at the reception of the hotel; the dress he wore was a bit similar to Army dress. After seeing him, Aashi stopped.

She left my hand and saluted him, saying loudly, *"Jai jawan jai kisan"*.

After seeing Aashi shouting like this, I couldn't stop myself from laughing.

The guard had seen both of us, but couldn't have afforded to say anything in front of us.

I dragged Aashi away from there and opened the room. Suddenly, Aashi vomited on me.

"Oh my god, Aashi, I told you not to drink that much." It seemed I had taken a bath with vomit. The worst moment I saw in my life and I picked Aashi in my lap and put her on the bed. I made myself comfortable and was thinking what to do.

I was just moving towards the bathroom to take shower when Aashi stood up and ran towards the bathroom. I thought she would puke again. But she came back with a bucket full of water, drained all the water on me, and shouted, "Happy Holi, Neev".

The entire room was full of water now. Without doing anything else, I sat where I had stood and was totally confused. But thank god, after celebrating Holi, Aashi slept, albeit on the floor itself.

I was shivering due to the cold monsoon of Goa. Still, I took the bath as Aashi had puked on me. After taking the bath, I picked up Aashi in my lap again and made her sleep comfortably on the bed.

I was feeling tired and within fifteen minutes, I dosed off.

I woke up early in the morning with a phone call from Aadi. He was asking me about the days I was spending in Dadri and I continued my lie that I am staying in a hotel and will be back in a few days.

He interrupted me and said, "I have to give you a surprise."

"Yes Aadi, tell me, what kind of surprise?"

"As you had told me, I have booked a plot for you in Agra. It was at a great location, so I paid the advance. Hope you will like that."

"Of course, yaar. If you have chosen it, I am sure I will like it. I will come as soon as possible now; I am really excited to see that plot."

Aadi had not discussed the matter with his parents.

I disconnected the phone and looked at Aashi; she was still fast asleep. Suddenly Aashi's phone started ringing; I saw it was from Nisha.

I woke her up and asked her to talk. I moved towards the bathroom to freshen up. When I came back, she was still talking to Nisha and suddenly, she gave the phone to me saying Nisha wanted to talk to me.

"Hello Nisha, how are you?"

"I am fine Neev. How about you?"

"All well, but we are missing you a lot."

"Aww me too. So when you are coming back?"

"Yeah we have already had a lot of fun here, so just planning to come back within two days."

"Great, I am waiting. Come soon, bye Neev."

When I disconnected the phone, I saw Aashi sitting on the floor with her hands joined.

I asked her what was wrong. She started apologising, "I am sorry baby. I know last night I had troubled you a lot."

"Yeah you are right, but it's okay. Leave that as I promised you, we have to go to see the beach."

She got ready to go within a few minutes. Aashi had been really excited for the beach from the very beginning.

We booked a taxi from the hotel Reception for the Calungate beach. The beach looked more beautiful because the sand was of golden colour and the beach is also known as "Golden Beach". As told by the hotel staff, it was the famous beach of Goa and mostly all tourists visited it. The taxi driver dropped us at the beach and asked me to call him when we would want to go back. Before leaving us, he asked us to be careful – "It is rainy season, sir, so don't go into the water. The tides are high; they can be dangerous". I was fully satisfied with the statement given by the driver and decided to follow that. After seeing the beach, Aashi's face lit up. As we got closer to the beach, Aashi held my hand hard due to fear of high tides. Many people were taking bath and enjoying at the beach. We removed our shoes and stood on the beach to feel the water. Earlier itself I had warned Aashi not to get closer to that. She was following my instructions and suddenly she said, "Why are we scared? We should enjoy. I don't know whether I will come here again or not. I want to enjoy these tides, Neev."

I gave her an angry look and said no.

She was again pleading with me. Knowing fully well how stubborn she was, I knew she would never listen to me. I didn't answer and was enjoying the cold water.

And suddenly Aashi left my hand and got a step back. I turned my head back and asked, "What happened?"

She pushed me into the water and I was totally soaked with the tide that just came in. I stood up and held Aashi; she was busy laughing me. I picked her in my lap, she was shouting, "No Neev. Don't do this; I am sorry." I took a few steps forward and put her down in the water. She was laughing so hard and I was busy in laughing at her. But this was really unexpected; she had her hands full of sand and she was running to put that on me. I was running a few steps far and she was running behind me. All the people were seeing us and suddenly Aashi jumped on me. I couldn't balance myself and fell down on the ground, but it didn't hurt me because the area was fully covered by sand only. Aashi made me lie down under her. She sat on my stomach and started putting sand on my face, on the head and inside the clothes. I was begging Aashi to stop as it was really horrible to have sand everywhere on the body; but I was enjoying when Aashi was doing this.

Many people had begun to record our video. After a few minutes of fun and rubbing sand all over me, she left me. I didn't think of doing the same to Aashi because people were noticing. We enjoyed the place for another couple of hours and then decided to go back. We called our taxi and asked him to go back to the hotel. He safely left us at the hotel. Aashi ordered the food as we bathed and got ready to eat.

We decided to get back to Bangalore the very next day, as we had seen most of the tourist spots. From the hotel reception itself, we booked our tickets to Bangalore.

We were enjoying the last day in the room and suddenly there was a shooting pain right below my stomach. I didn't notice that till it became unbearable. I shared this with Aashi; she called up the reception and asked for the nearest clinic. According to them, there was 55 years old Dr. Iyer who had a clinic right next to our hotel. I was not agreeing to go to the doctor, but Aashi forced me.

We moved to the clinic which welcomed us with a board that read: Dr. RAMESHWARAM IYER. We stepped inside the clinic; there were only two people sitting. In the front opposite to the table an old man was sitting and on the other side a lady aged around 30-35 years was sitting in the chair. I was sure that the old man was the doctor. I sat in the chair next to the lady. I told the doctor about my pain. He asked me to lie in the bed at the other corner of the room. I was happy to see the doctor because he looked experienced. But suddenly my pain increased manifold. I was not able to control the pain and started shouting, "Oh my god, it is paining a lot, doctor. Please do something, quick."

Aashi began to cry and came near me and said, "Don't worry, Neev, the doctor will make you feel better. Aashi asked, "What happened? Do something; can't you see he is in pain?"

He gave me three injections and said the pain is due to swollen liver, owing to excessive intake of. Don't worry; it will be normal within minutes."

First time I was feeling good because with this, I had a hope that I would be fine soon. The injection had no effect, though. Aashi had not left my hand all along. She was still having tears in her eyes. With one hand, I wiped all her tears. The doctor told me with a great confidence, "Just wait, the injection will work slowly."

The woman sitting in the clinic added, "You have come to the correct place. Dr. Iyer is the most intelligent doctor in this entire area."

Upon hearing this, Dr. Iyer had a big smile on his face. I was still having pain. Suddenly Aashi left my hand and moved towards the doctor; he was sitting comfortably in his chair.

"*Saale buddhe*, you gave him three injections, and still he is suffering from pain. What use is all your experience?"

The doctor was puzzled and was busy in finding courage to defend himself from Aashi's verbal attack. He repeated his sentence, "Don't worry, madam. I have given him the injections; it will take a few minutes to get better."

Just then, the middle-aged lady also stood up and consoled Aashi, "Have patience dear, the doctor has given the treatment; it will take some time."

Aashi was frustrated with that woman also and shouted at her as I lay there in pain, "Please keep quiet! It's none of your business. Just give me the address of the nearest hospital. I am not going to stay here for a minute."

The doctor was angry and turned his face as he felt insulted.

And just then I realised that my pain was gone. The doctor had been right all along. I was fine now. There was no trace of pain. I told Aashi, "I am fine now, baby."

Aashi looked at me and kissed me on my cheeks. Her eyes were filled with tears. I stood up from the bed and asked doctor, "Will it occur again doctor?"

He shouted at me and said, "Just get lost! You cheap people don't deserve any treatment." None of us argued with the doctor because we were at fault and he was very angry; it meant sure trouble for us. We left the place as soon as possible. I knew too well that Aashi was wrong and she should have been more patient; maybe seeing me as a patient did that to her. Anyway, it was too late for anything now, so I apologised to the doctor and the lady briefly and left.

The moment we came out of the clinic, I started laughing at Aashi. She was still crying. I hugged her. Both of us left for our hotel.

We had our bus for Bangalore early the next morning. We were sleeping in the bed, next to each other when suddenly Aashi put her right hand on my chest. I picked her hand with both my hands. Aashi came closer to my face and kissed me on my forehead; she was crying.

I was shocked and asked, "What has happened to you, baby?"

"Neev, I don't want to go anywhere. I want to live with you forever. I don't know why but I have a lingering fear in my heart. It seems that these are the last days of my life with you."

"Shut up, Aashi. Don't say anything. I am not going to leave you ever." I came closer to her and kissed her. We forgot all our worries of being separated in the future and made love. I was spending those moments of love, which we might not be lucky to get again. We both were crazy for each other.

Next morning, we reached to bus stand on time.

We didn't give any notice to Nisha, as we had decided to give her a surprise. That is why we had booked our tickets for the morning, so that we would find Nisha in the evening.

After about eight hours of travel, we reached Bangalore bus stand and took a taxi for Nisha's home. It took around fifteen minutes from there to her home. At the same time we received a call from Nisha, but we were excited and wanted to give her a surprise, so we didn't receive the call.

Aashi was sure Nisha would be too excited to see us.

We knocked the door and were ready to say loudly, "Surprise!"

We both were hiding on the sides of the door, ready to shout at her the moment she opened the door.

And when the gate was about to open and we shouted "Surprise", the response was shocking: "Neev and Aashi?"

To our surprise, it was not Nisha. It was Aadi. It was *Aadi*. We both were shocked and puzzled after seeing him. We could not make ourselves comfortable and then we saw Aashi's parents also.

I was shivering with fear by now. I was sure it wasn't a dream as I could see everything clearly. I was not in a situation to react. Aadi was standing in front me and his parents were still not aware of us. Aashi was looking at me and Aadi was staring at us with anger, shock and surprise. Somewhere inside me, I had been preparing myself to face all these things, but I never thought it'd be so soon.

Beauty of love had disappeared for a moment for me because Aadi was also a very dear friend. Knowing all these things how would he react, I didn't want to imagine. In real sense, I had betrayed him. But both the relations at stake were very precious to me; whether Aashi, my love, now my life; or Aadi my friend, who was an epitome of true friendship in my life. I loved both of them so much. If somebody asked me to "choose one out of the two", it would have been like choosing between both my eyes. It was an awkward situation for me. Every moment I was thinking how I will convince Aadi and his parents; how they will react. For a moment, my entire world had stopped and I was standing there like a stone. It was a feeling of having been caught red handed. And none could have saved us from the anger of Aadi and his parents.

9

LOVE, PARENTS OR LOVE

Sometimes it is difficult to narrate the situation you're in or what you are feeling. As I stood in front of Aadi, even I blanked out.

Suddenly I head uncle's voice from inside, asking Aadi who was at the door. Even he was too frightened or shocked to say anything and stepped back. Nisha was standing in the kitchen, having her mobile in her hand. Apparently, she had not noticed us. Aadi's parents stood up from their place and came towards the door. We were still standing at the gate and Aashi had tears in her eyes. She was afraid of the situation.

Both Aunty and uncle saw us and came near us. They were puzzled after seeing us. But the figure was clear in their mind.

Uncle roared like a lion, "Neev, what are you doing here?" Suddenly Nisha heard the sound and ran towards us. I was puzzled in front of them to say something. Nisha came and stood next to Aashi.

Aadi was standing behind uncle and aunty. Aunty took a step forward and gave me a tight slap. But in true meaning, it was the hand of a mother, who spent lots of years with her daughter and now I stood in between them. I deserved this slap. I didn't react to this. Aunty moved ahead to slap Aashi also, at which she started crying loudly. Nisha stopped aunty and said, "Don't do this!"

Uncle reprimanded her, "You shut up, Nisha".

"Sorry, uncle," were the first words that came out of my mouth.

Aadi took a few steps and just said a single sentence, "I didn't expect this from you, Neev."

I had tears in my eyes. Aashi added, "We love each other."

"Shut up, you bitch! This is what you gave in place of our trust?" Aunty was very angry, and turned towards me, "And you, Neev, how could you do this? Did you forget everything we did for you?"

"Aunty, I am sorry. Whatever I did was wrong, but uncle please try to understand me. I love Aashi and I want to marry her," I managed to say between sobs.

The great Indian mother came forward, "Do you deserve our daughter? You don't deserve to stand in front of us and you are talking of marrying our girl?"

What could I say to that; I always knew this will be brought up at the first instance of confrontation, "Aunty, I know I am nothing in front of you, except my love for Aashi."

Aashi gathered herself to say, "Yes mom, we both love each other and I can't survive without him."

"Neev, do you know what you are saying? We are *brahmins* and you are Singh. You don't have a family; not a single person who could be known as your family. You are like an insect, how can you marry my daughter?" Uncle said.

After hearing the last statement, I was shocked. My tears were falling down from the eyes and Aashi was in the same condition. I was feeling guilty for what I had done. But my love was true and I wanted to marry her.

Aunty held Aashi's hand and moved back towards the room. Uncle followed them. I didn't know what to do, how to react, or where to go? The condition was similar to when I had lost my father. After remembering my dad, my tears started rolling down faster.

Aadi came forward as his parents went in and said to me, "Stop your drama of crying. I had no idea about you. It's hard to believe, that you stabbed me like this. Was there anything I did wrong with you? You have cheated me. I can't forgive you, Neev."

"Aadi I am sorry, but please try to understand. I love Aashi, I can't live without her."

He put a paper and pen and wrote something. He handled me the paper and said, "This is the address of your plot and there are two rooms built on it. I will tell the owner to take the money from you. We will send all your stuff to your new house; don't ever come to our home. I don't want to see your face."

I took the paper and started begging in front of Aadi, "Please Aadi, forgive me. I know I am wrong, but please try to understand that I love Aashi. You know me well, Aadi, I don't commit anything easily. I really love her, yaar. I am not able to live a single moment without her."

Aadi turned to me in anger and disgust, "Neev, just go! Please don't force me to do something wrong with you, I hate you. I am still behaving like a kind person with you just because you were my friend."

"Aadi, please listen to me..."

Nisha was still standing there and added, "Aadi, he is right. He loves her and Aashi loves him too."

I was looking at Nisha and suddenly Aadi pushed me towards the gate. And he shut the gate on my face. I sat on the same place and was thinking of Aashi. I couldn't stop my tears. I was empty handed because my luggage was inside the gate. I stood up to move. I got down from the stairs and took a taxi to the airport. I reached the airport and booked a ticket for Delhi. I flew back in an hour.

While on the flight, I was reminded of the last time I was flying. I was so excited and curious about everything. But this time, I had tears in my eyes. I was missing Aashi. It felt as if I had left a part of my body back in Bangalore. I was thinking about the time when I was at Nisha's home. I was still feeling guilty for everything.

When I thought of Aashi, I was sure I didn't do anything wrong; but at the same time, I had cheated the whole family. I had cheated those people who had stood by me when the world had deserted me. Even my kin had not come to my rescue when these people had. I should have been thankful to them for a lifetime, but instead of that, I had broken their trust. I had cheated Aadi who called me his best friend, who had given me a job, a place to stay. More than a friend, he had helped me like a brother.

On the one hand was this girl I loved with all my soul, even more than myself. On the other hand, I had a family who felt cheated by me. I wanted to marry her. I was prepared to give love to her till my last breath. I was even ready to beg in front of them. I could have given up anything for her; anything for her, yaar.

I am a human being and I need love. I saw that love in Aashi when I needed it the most; so she became my life. If it is wrong to love one's own life, then I should be punished.

Upon landing in Delhi, I hopped on to an Agra-bound bus from Sarai Kale Khan bus stand. I was thinking what they were doing with Aashi. I had called Nisha many times, also Aashi and Aadi; none of them had responded. I was afraid for Aashi. How is she? I was worried because everyone would have been very angry and they could have hurt Aashi. But except crying, I had no option. I was just praying to god, to keep her safe.

Some of the situations are so typical that we don't understand who can help us. I was about to reach Agra and I picked up the same piece of paper given by Aadi. After seeing that paper I again felt sad; how wrong I had been to Aadi, when he did so many things for me. I befooled him; I cheated him. I don't know what was written in my future but for one thing that god will definitely punish me, whether I will get Aashi or not was for cheating on Aadi. At some places, I was wrong.

I asked the bus conductor to drop me at the bus stop nearest to the place written on that paper. He advised me to take an auto-rickshaw from the bus stand itself. The good thing about Agra is that at every corner, you will find auto-rickshaw. I was empty handed but had lots of pain in my heart. I took an auto and reached that place. I paid the price to the driver and saw the lock on the gate. A ten year old boy ran towards me and shouted, "Are you Neev bhaiya?"

I nodded and said, "Yes". The boy had come out from the neighbour's house.

He replied, "Aadi bhaiya had called just now and asked to give these keys to you."

At the same moment, after hearing the line from the boy I couldn't stop myself to cry for Aadi.

The boy handed those keys to me and ran back to the house; his mother was waiting for him at the gate.

I opened the front door and saw something written with flowers on the front porch of the house. Due to bad light, I couldn't see what was written; I searched for the light switch. I switched on the light and saw: WELCOME NEEV.

I began feeling more guilty after seeing this; I couldn't stop myself from crying. I sat down at the same place and put my hand on my head. I was feeling horrible at having cheated Aadi, such a good friend.

The plot had two rooms with a kitchen and a toilet built; the rest of it was empty. There was a lot of empty apace on the plot. It was similar to what I wished to have. I had planned to fulfil Aashi's dream of opening an animal shelter on this plot.

But I stopped thinking more about that dream, because the dreamer was not with me. I was thinking of Aashi, hoping she was fine. I was more worried for her because she was stubborn and could do anything. I was afraid that she shouldn't take any wrong steps.

Just then, my phone buzzed. Curiously, I checked and it was an sms from Nisha: "We all are coming back to Agra, Aashi is fine. Hope you've found your place and sorry Neev they all came suddenly and surprised me."

I was a bit relaxed, but still I was missing Aashi immensely. I was also unsure about my future, because in a so short period of time, I had faced things that were just as unpredictable. I was living with the hope that something good was to happen. My soul was not ready to accept that I had lost Aashi. Somewhere in my heart, I could hear, "My love is true and I will get her." On the other side I also had a fear that her parents and Aadi will never allow me to get married to her. I had decided to wait for a few days. The day when I feel there will be good environment to talk, then I will try once to talk to her parents.

I do not have any other clothes to change, so I felt comfortable to sleep in the same dress on the floor itself because the house was empty, without any furniture.

I was looking outside my room and was thinking about the moon. How beautiful it is; exactly like my love. I don't know what would she be thinking right now; but I was sure she must be thinking about me.

I didn't realise when I slept off, thinking about Aashi.

Next day, at around 11:00 a.m., while I was still sleeping, there was a knock on the door.

I was surprised as to who it would be. When I opened the door, someone rushed towards me and hugged me. I couldn't even see who it was.

"I am sorry, Neev," it was Aadi.

"What happened, Aadi?"

I looked behind him, towards the gate; all my luggage was there. I felt relaxed after seeing that. Somehow I calmed Aadi down and asked him, "Why you are saying sorry, Aadi? I should be saying sorry to you."

"Neev, I read your personal diary yesterday in the flight. Sorry for that, but it was a coincidence. I thought it was some magazine due to the attractive cover.

"Aadi, it's okay dear."

"After reading your feelings, I feel your love for Aashi is very pure and true. I should have given you a chance to speak yesterday. Why didn't you tell me earlier that you loved her so much? I have always shared every little thing with you." His eyes were questioning me and I had no answer, so he continued, "Neev, I am sorry for my parents. I talked to Aashi also; she told me how much you love each other. I am sorry for my behaviour yesterday."

I was touched, "Aadi, I don't know what you are saying." But in my heart, I was very happy. As for me, Aadi's support was a great achievement.

"Neev, now don't think anything else; just remember I am with you. I will talk to mom and dad."

The only thing going on in my mind was about the benefits of writing a diary; at the same time, I pledged to continue with this habit.

Aadi suggested me to visit home once in the evening, and talk to his parents for Aashi.

I was surprised that Aadi had suggested such a thing, despite his parents' having warned me but a few hours back.

Both of us chuckled but he told me it could still work out.

"Okay, as you wish Aadi. No one else would have guided me the way you have, not today, but throughout my tough time. I will be there in the evening at 5:00 p.m. sharp."

Aadi went back home after leaving my luggage. I was a bit relaxed after seeing Aadi standing in my support. I know very well that Aadi could do anything for me.

I was standing alone in the house and just looking at the watch in my hand.

It was 12:15 pm. I had to be there at 5:00 p.m. The first thing was to plan what exactly I had to speak in front of Aashi's parents.

I had prepared a note to learn and frequently speak in front of her parents with full emotions. I was a bit nervous because this was my last chance to convince them. I was crossing their last warning, which they had given me in Bangalore. Only one thing was giving me confidence – Aashi's love. I don't know what they would prefer more – caste or their daughter.

I was nervous even before leaving for their house. I had the fear of losing Aashi. I was very curious to see Aashi, because I had not talked to her after coming back from Bangalore.

Once again, before going to Aashi's house, I spoke to Aadi over phone and asked him to talk to his parents and try to convince them.

I wore the same shirt over which Aashi had sprayed ink once.

I knocked at their door and suddenly I received a message on my cell from Aadi, "Come around 8:00 p.m., I have not talked to mom and dad yet". By the time I finished reading the text, Aashi's father had opened the door.

I was afraid because Aadi hadn't talk to them till now.

Uncle saw me and started shouting, "Why have you come here?"

In the most pleading manner I said, "Uncle I just want to talk to you once."

"Get lost! I do not have any time for you."

"Uncle, please, it's about my life, about Aashi's life," I was pleading.

I noticed that he became slightly nervous after hearing Aashi's name. Every father has a wish that his daughter should settle down.

I added, "Uncle, just once I want to talk you, after that whatever you decide for us, we will follow that."

Suddenly Aadi rushed out, as he was unaware that I was standing at the gate.

Aadi added, "Yes dad, he is as nice guy. Please listen to him once."

Surprisingly, a voice came, "*Ab kya bacha hai? Dono ne naak to kata hi di hai.* What does he want to discuss now after insulting and hurting us the way he has."

Exactly the comment that one would expect from "the great Indian mother" in such a situation.

Nisha came in front and said to aunty, "Please aunty, let him speak his heart out once."

Uncle allowed me to come inside.

I saw towards Aashi's window, she was standing there.

A few chairs were placed in the hall itself and we all sat there, while Aashi looked on from her window.

I was shivering completely, but this was my last chance, so I had to talk to them and convince them for marriage. For me, it was a win or win condition.

I stood up from my chair and started my speech,

"Uncle ji and Aunty ji, first of all I want to say sorry to you. I know I was wrong everywhere. I still remember the day when both of you came to my room and said, 'Beta don't think that you are alone; we are always with you.' That was the day when I felt that god sent my parents back. I don't remember my mom, as at a very young age I lost her."

I was noticing that everyone was listening to me very carefully.

So I continued,

"After coming from Dadri, I met all of you. The love that I got from you all can't be expressed in words. I felt so blessed. I never ate food late; aunty always gave me food on time. It was like a miracle for me. I was puzzled with my life, how can I get two parents in one life. At the same moment I want to tell both of you that you are not like my parents, you are more than my parents.

"Uncle ji and Aunty ji, there is someone who is more than you both for me, and that is Aashi. I love her more than my soul. At every moment, I feel I can't live without her. She has become my life. With every heartbeat, I miss her. It is possible for me to make distance with my soul, but with Aashi, it's really impossible.

"I know it was never a matter of love for you; it's a matter of society, religion and what people will say. You will be more proud in front of people if she marries a boy of upper caste; but have you ever thought of Aashi's happiness? If she takes any drastic step, what will you do?

"I never wish that something like this happens in future. I know I am not a perfect guy in this world for Aashi, but uncle ji I assure you that I will never allow Aashi to be sad. I will never allow tears in reach her eyes. I will love her at every moment."

I had finished talking and had tears in my eyes. I stepped back to see Aashi in the window. She was still standing at the window listening to everything. Her tears were visible to me from that distance also.

I made myself sit in the chair, Aashi's mom had tears in her eyes, Aadi was normal, Nisha had tears in her eyes. And the main victim was left and that was Aashi's dad. He was really a kind person. I was afraid of him only.

Aashi's father stood up from his chair and said, "Nice speech!"

I didn't reply anything.

"Have you ever thought for what you have come in this world?"

I was blank; I didn't reply. Sometimes it's better to get zero marks in oral examination so I kept quiet.

He saw that I was silent, so he continued, "We all have come to this world to do something good. And it was our elders who made this caste system to maintain a particular disciplined way of life. Why don't you think of marrying in the same caste? As you said you are in love, why did you fall in love with her in the first place when you knew she is from another upper caste? There are many things except her to notice in this world. I know you will ask me why we are allowing Aadi to marry in other caste then. Have you ever thought how I will face the society? No one would like to have food with me ever. The people who have no guts to speak in front of me, they will make fun of me. I don't believe in your love Neev, and I would never allow my daughter to marry you.

"You can't ever think of the problems we will face after your marriage with Aashi.

So it's my humble request to you, please get out of my house and never think of being with Aashi ever in life, if you have some respect for us.

My eyes were full of tears; the condition was similar as when we lose someone. Everything was over for me, I didn't see any hope. I was puzzled as to what should I do next. I remember all the things did by uncle and aunty. Today, they were asking me to leave their daughter in return of all that.

Surprisingly, I heard a noise from where Aashi's window was. I was more nervous now because she is a nut. She is standing at the same window, which faces towards us.

She roared like a lion and said, "I was watching you all for one hour; it was a good conversation. Both of you really did a great job. Neev thank you for being my love, and dad, you are awesome. You have already planned what people will think of you. Did you think even once what your daughter will do if she doesn't get her love?"

There was pin drop silence in the hall below and rooms above. Then suddenly Aashi roared once more.

"Wait, I will tell you what she can do."

She went beyond the window, so we couldn't see her for a few seconds, and then she reappeared. She shouted yet again, "I have locked my room and you all can see this bottle in my hand. Hope it is visible to you all. If not, don't worry, I will tell you. Liquid mosquito destroyer."

After hearing this, Aashi's mom shouted, "Oh god, now this!"

She addressed her, "Yes mom, you are right. This is the only thing which is left now. Listen carefully everyone, I love Neev and will love Neev till my last breath and I will marry none other than him.

"Neev, if you have some problem, please let me know and dad, I am asking you again, will you allow me to marry Neev or not? I know very well that Neev won't marry me till you give your consent. So I will count till five, and will drink this liquid. Till the time you come to me, I will be gone forever."

I was shocked at this sudden development, and knew Aashi too well to take this as a simple threat.

"One."

"Aashi, stop it! Don't do this, please. We will talk to uncle together, come downstairs," I shouted.

"Two."

Aadi ran towards her room; her mother was sobbing uncontrollably and Nisha was trying to calm her down, shedding tears herself.

"Three."

Uncle shouted, "Beta please try to understand…"

We could hear Aadi banging her door, but it was tightly shut and locked from the inside.

"Four."

Nisha and I shouted, "Please Aashi, it would be dangerous. Don't be a fool."

I couldn't believe what she was doing. I said again, "Aashi baby, I have loved you so much, Don't do this to me. If something happens to you, what will I do?"

We all had tears in our eyes. I was looking at uncle, he was shivering. I couldn't manage myself to say something to him and I was so shocked with this act of Aashi's. My tears were just rolling down my cheeks, and my eyes were completely glued to Uncle ji's lips. Aashi had counted till four already, and I was scared of the consequences if uncle did not stop her himself.

"Five!"

"Stop, Aashi! Do whatever you want to do. I agree with you." Uncle finally said it.

I looked at Aashi; she had a smile on her face. But suddenly, she dropped that liquid bottle and it fell. I was confused why she was reacting like this, now that her father had agreed. Had she drunk it before uncle said it?

Aashi couldn't manage herself and fell down on the floor.

Everyone ran towards her room to see what had gone wrong. I saw Aadi still busy in breaking the door. I heard Nisha shout, "Aadi, break the door. I think Aashi has consumed the poison."

I was confused in all this chaos, and was running as fast as I could. In my heart, there was unending, immeasurable love for this stubborn girl; in my mind, there was a constant fear of losing her. I was shivering thinking what had happened to her.

Love is a divine power. It is created by god. Love is a beautiful feeling in itself. However, to fall in love is different and to be lucky enough to be able to be with them forever is different.

Love should not be short-lived. It should be never-ending, spontaneous, flawless and blessed by Almighty.

10

SOMEONE WHO WAS NEVER MINE

Whatever life gives us, we have to accept – it could be happiness or grief. We ought to live every moment of life, though not sure what we will be getting.

With me, the unexpected had happened.

I was scared for Aashi. Aadi was still busy in breaking the door and I was watching him. Just then, Uncle ji came with a hammer and gave me.

He was impatient for her daughter; he instructed that they should break the door using that hammer. I could see the immense pain and fear in his eyes for his daughter; he was a father, he couldn't have seen his daughter getting hurt. Ethics, morals, society, reputation – all vanish. They forget everything when it stands against their children.

I picked up the hammer and took some step forward towards the gate. I asked Aadi to give some space; I hit the door some four-five times gathering all my energy and the door latch broke open. Aunty ji and Nisha ran towards Aashi. They saw Aashi lying on the floor.

Nisha was rubbing Aashi's palms but she was not responding to that. Aadi came forward, picked her in his lap, and asked me to get going to the hospital.

I didn't respond to Aadi. My tears were rolling down. I feared if Aashi had drunk the mosquito destroyer.

Aadi gave me a push and asked me to be quick.

I nodded and Aadi gave Aashi over to me, himself running to bring the neighbour's car. Within two minutes, he brought the car and asked me to sit with Aashi in the car. Everyone present was so nervous, that no one had anything to say. Everyone was just following Aadi's command. I made Aashi lie down on the back seat of the car. Aashi's dad sat in front while Aadi drove.

As we rolled out, Uncle told Aunty and Nisha, "Don't worry, I will call after sometime."

I was sitting at the back with Aashi, my hand was on Aashi's forehead and tears had filled my eyes. My legs were shivering due to the fear of losing Aashi.

Aadi was driving the car and simultaneously he was discussing with his dad in which hospital they should take her to. He said some "Ajay Narang Hospital" situated nearby. The hospital is known for its best globally equipped doctors and instruments. Both of them decided to go to the same hospital as it was about ten minutes away only, while all others were father off. I was praying to god for Aashi.

We reached the hospital; the entrance gate itself proved that the hospital was globally known. I felt relaxed that definitely we will get positive result here. Uncle ji got off the car and asked Aadi to park the car. Till now I had Aashi in my lap and I was following Aashi's dad in the hospital. After seeing us, one of the ward boys came with the moving stretcher and asked me to put Aashi on that. I put Aashi on that and held her hand. On the other side, another ward boy was asking to fill the form, "How has it happened?"

They shifted Aashi to the ICU. From the glass door, everything was visible. It was a team of four doctors inside. They had covered Aashi from almost all sides. I was nervous and asked one of the ward boys, "What's going on inside? Please tell me."

I was sobbing uncontrollably, and Aadi and Uncle ji were also standing next to me, teary-eyed.

The ward boy answered, "The doctor will tell you."

After some ten odd minutes, one of the doctors came outside and I excused him, "Sir, how is she? What has happened to her?"

He was calm, but disturbed, "We haven't found out yet what has happened to her. Everything is normal," and he moved to the other cabin to take some instruments.

After hearing the doctor's last words, we were shocked as to what had happened to her. Aashi's father asked me to tell the doctors that she must have consumed some poisonous liquid. It will be helpful for them.

I knocked at the door; one of the doctors came out and I shared the news of the liquid mosquito destroyer.

In response, the doctor told me that they could not find anything poisonous that she could have drunk to make her collapse the way she did.

I couldn't move my eyes from the ICU ward for a single second.

Suddenly, I saw Nisha and Aunti ji coming. The first question they asked Aadi sitting in the chair was, "How is she?"

"Doctors have not found the cause until now."

After hearing this, they both had tears in their eyes. Aunty ji had folded her hands- prayed to god, usually we all do when there is no option left.

I was still busy watching Aashi from that glass door of the ICU.

Aashi had been wired to the several monitors with respect to different body parts, to have a view of every body part whether it's working accurately or not. After seeing her like this, tears were rolling down my cheeks.

Surprisingly, one of the doctors started pulling out the entire attached instrument from Aashi's body. I couldn't gather what they were doing.

One of the doctors signed the rest of the team to send Aashi out. After seeing her signs making towards the gate, I was shivering whether something unusual has happened. Then one of the ward boys standing at the corner took some steps in the room and started moving the stretcher. The ward boy took Aashi out of the room. When he opened the door, I asked him what has happened.

He answered, "I don't know. Doctor sahib has ordered me to have CT scan of the entire body done."

I allowed him to go fast, without wasting any more time.

I was moving with the stretcher and the rest of the family was sitting in the chairs in front of ICU ward. I held Aashi's hand, but she had no idea what I was doing.

For me, it was difficult to look anywhere else when I was in front of Aashi. We had to take Aashi to the lower floor, so I went with them. When we were just about to get into the lift, surprisingly Aashi opened her eyes. I saw and mumbled slowly to let the ward boy get to know. When the ward boy touched Aashi's wrist to feel the beats, Aashi put her hand on the fore hand and started shouting.

She started throwing her legs and hands in different directions. For me, it was difficult to know what exactly she was doing. The ward boy stopped the stretcher and started moving in the opposite direction to reach the ICU again. Aashi was shouting, "Oh my god, it's paining so bad. Ohm, help me...aaah!" It was difficult to hold her, I don't know from where she got so much energy. I was busy in holding her shoulder at the stretcher. She was throwing her legs and arms continuously. After hearing Aashi's voice, all the family members rushed towards me. They all became nervous after seeing her like this. After hearing so much noise, one of the doctors shouted to give anaesthesia to her. The other doctor did his work as fast as he could; he gave an injection to Aashi and within a few minutes, Aashi drifted back to sleep.

The head of the doctors told the other one to have CT scan of the brain done fast.

Within half an hour they got the reports. The doctor called us into his cabin. Aashi was still unconscious. It was obvious that there was something fishy in the reports. Continuously, I was praying to god to give some positive result. We all entered the cabin.

The doctor asked us to sit in the chairs. We all took our chairs.

The Doctor asked us, "How many times had she had an attack like this?"

Aunty quickly said, "It was her first time."

The doctor was worried, "It's not possible. The reports are clearly showing that she had pain for a long time."

Uncle ji said, "Yes, she told us many times that she was having pain in her head. But we never took it seriously. She took some pain killer and it would be fine."

I was sure that the doctor was discussing the same, which Aashi used to have in college and several times at home.

The doctor shouted, "What do you mean by some medicine? Do you know those kinds of medicines give relief for some time only? You know the reason for such pain?"

There was silence in the cabin.

"She has a tumour in the brain; which has reached its final stage now due to your ignorance."

Aadi asked innocently, "What is a brain tumour, sir?"

The doctor calmed down and explained, "Brain tumour is life threatening, the symptoms depend on the size, types and location of the tumour. Headaches are usually worse. Secondly changes in moods, personality, or ability to concentrate. It is almost like cancer in the brain. It could have been controlled through treatment, if you had taken it seriously earlier."

Nisha asked, "What do you mean by could have been controlled?"

The doctor looked at her sympathetically and said, "I mean, it's difficult to save her now. The brain cancer had reached its last level. Now we can only *try* to save her. But practically, the patient does not have too much time."

I was heartbroken, and was cursing myself to have not taken Aashi to a doctor by force. In the meantime, Uncle ji asked, "How much time does she have?"

"We can't say anything; it depends on god. But we are sure she will not live long."

It was the most tragic thing I had ever heard after my dad's death. I was broken from inside, tears falling down, I was feeling like a mountain had fallen on me or I was drowning deep in the ocean and could not breathe.

I stood up at the same moment and got near the ICU. The door was not locked and only a ward boy was sitting inside. I entered the room and asked him to move outside. I was looking terrible, the ward boy left without saying a word.

I was sitting on the floor and was watching Aashi. Her left hand was hanging out of the bed. I picked her hand and kissed on the wrist, crying. It seemed I had nothing left in this world. I was mubling while crying, "How could you do this to me, Aashi? You had promised to marry me."

For me, it was the same situation I faced when my dad left me alone. I was shouting now, "Aashi, please wake up and hug me, baby. Don't leave me alone; I can't live without you, my love." Her moments, of love, naughtiness, care, affection and madness were revolving in my mind, making me go crazy at the very thought of losing her.

After remembering this, I took her hand close to my heart and shouted, "I will not let you go, Aashi. There is no one without you. I need you every second. I stood up and sat on the bed next to Aashi. My tears were getting down on Aashi's hand. I was still crying loudly and suddenly the door opened. It was Aashi's mom and dad. They had come to me and put their hand on my back. I saw them, they too had tears in their eyes.

They told me, "Don't worry Neev, she will be fine."

"No she will not. I know her; she always hurts me. She never listens to me. I need her in my life and that is why she is teasing me. She is stubborn, very stubborn."

Auntie's hands were on my eyes, wiping my tears.

Aadi and Nisha entered the room. Aadi said, "Are you mad? Be strong. Just now, the doctor told me that Aashi would be fine."

I knew he was lying, I hugged Aadi and mumbled, "Aadi, you are my best friend. Please do something."

After hearing this, he couldn't stop himself and cried. From the other side, Nisha came closer to us and hugged both of us. Nisha too started crying loudly.

It was difficult for me stop crying. We all loved her immensely to be able to endure this pain.

Suddenly a ward boy came inside, and told all of us to move outside the room and we did.

I was sitting and was thinking about Aashi. In front of me there was another pair of chairs. One of the chairs was empty. The man who was sitting had lost both his hands in an accident. His situation and mine seemed similar to me. He was forced to be handicapped, and I did not feel like doing anything in this world.

It was around 1:00 am. I told all of them to go home and have food while I'd stay with Aashi.

Aunty ji told me to go home, and she decided to stay back in the hospital.

I announced, "I will not be going anywhere tonight and will have food from the canteen. So you all just go and relax at home. Tomorrow also is going to be a long day."

They made my decision final and Aadi asked me to call him whenever I needed.

I got back to those chairs. I was feeling a bit cold in the night. I was searching for a blanket in the hospital and remembered the time when in the beginning Aashi bought me a blanket in the night. I sat at the same place and started mumbling, "Aashi please bring me a blanket. I need one."

I was crying loudly and simultaneously I was seeing around me whether someone was noticing me or not. But the positive result was there was no one waking on the entire floor. I was missing Aashi a lot. It was like I was missing my heart beats. I was shivering due to cold and seeing me shivering, the ward boy sitting inside the ICU called me inside.

When he called me in, Aashi was sleeping.

I was reminded of the last days my dad spent in the hospital. God made me alone at that time. He made me alone in the world. But at the same instant, he had gifted me Aashi to love and to be loved. She took all my sorrows and converted all those into happiness. She is the one who has taught me how to live in this world. She is the one for whom I had knitted dreams and she was important for me. So important that I had only one dream, to fulfil all her dreams.

The time I was thinking about her, I was remembering the earlier phase of life which I spent with her. A dream of Aashi was clicking in my mind again and again. The only dream which she wanted to fulfil anyhow was to make an animal shelter for homeless animals. I decided to complete that work before Aashi leaves this world.

It was around 3:00 a.m. and in front of me Aashi was still sleeping due to anaesthesia given to her. I woke up the ward boy and asked him to tell me the truth, "How many days will she live for?"

He was shattered and puzzled after seeing me so desperate; plus at such an unearthly hour in the day.

He shook his head and said, "I am not sure, but she'll definitely not live more than two or three days as she has reached the final stage." A drop of tear came from my eyes. For me that ward boy was like the worst person of my life. But I had to accept the truth.

I came near Aashi, put a hand on her forehead and mumbled, "Please come back, love."

I was waiting for morning desperately. According to the doctor, Aashi will be normal by morning; the effect of the anaesthesia will be over by then.

The time Aashi woke up, Aadi knocked the door. As it was obvious he was too worried for her. It was around 5:00 am. He asked me, "Is everything fine?"

I replied, "She is the same."

After seeing us talking, the ward boy asked us to go out and talk.

We left the room and suddenly the ward boy went outside. He rushed towards the doctor's cabin. The situation itself was fishy. I didn't ask anything. I saw it was Aashi who was moving her eyebrows. She had opened her eyes. I had a smile on my face. I didn't enter the room because it was not allowed and I was sure if I reached near her then I would start crying again.

The doctor was available in his cabin; he was in a hurry to see Aashi. I was watching Aashi from the glass door. The doctor was asking something and Aashi was mumbling something, though it was not audible to me. There was some hope that Aashi might be fine. But whenever I remembered the words of the ward boy and doctors, my hope was shattered. The doctor had again attached some of the instruments and the monitors were showing some unusual graphs.

For another hour, he did some activities with those instruments.. I was waiting eagerly to hear some good news from the doctor. Finally, he came out.

I stood in front of him and asked, "How is she"?

The reports are not normal; the disease is in moving mode. Anytime it can hurt the brain as it did last night.

I added, "Is there any option to save her life?"

"No, if she gets another attack, she won't be able to survive it. We are giving medicines to her for some positive results."

I was crying; Aadi asked him if could we meet her.

"Yeah definitely. But please, not more than five minutes and talk one by one," he said strictly.

Both of us moved in. Aashi saw us and started smiling. The first question by her was, "How many days do you think I will live now? The doctor is saying I will live only 2-3 days."

Aadi said, "You will live a hundred years, sister."

I was feeling bad for her and couldn't stop crying. I was hiding my tears from Aashi.

Suddenly Aashi shouted, "Neev, I know you are crying; so don't hide from me. I want to see you till my last breath."

I came forward and held her hand, "Did I ever do any wrong with you? Why are you leaving me?" I was crying loudly. Aadi couldn't bear to see us like that and left the room.

Aashi pulled my hand towards her and asked me to hug her. She began crying with me. I was sleeping partially on her. She told me, "Neev, you know I am not happy that I am going to die. I am upset how you would manage after me. I don't want to die, I want to live for you forever."

We were crying loudly and the ward boy again interrupted. He shouted at me and said, "Patient needs rest, get out from here".

I woke up from her bed and held her hand, "Aashi please be fine for me; I can't live without you. The ward boy pulled me towards the gate and I left her hand. I was seeing Aashi was crying, just like all of us.

She said as I left, "I love you, Neev. I want to live for you." I heard her, couldn't manage to stop myself, rushed towards her, and hugged her, "Baby, don't leave me. I can't live without you."

This time Aadi came inside and asked me to come outside. He hugged me and said, "Please Neev, control yourself." I was still crying.

The time I was crying, I remembered the Aashi's dream. I had to complete it within time. Anyhow, I want Aashi to see that shelter. I told Aadi, "I have some work at home and I have to go".

He told me, "Okay, have some rest and take care of yourself, please."

It was around 8:00 a.m. in the morning; I rushed from the hospital and decided first to choose a guy who can make food for animals daily. I chose a farmer who knew what food was to be served to the cows, dogs and pigs. He came from a nearby village; I fixed his salary on a monthly basis.

According to my calculations, around ten animals could live there comfortably. I had decided to begin this with a small number of animals only.

I began my journey to pick those animals that have really less sources to have food in the city. In colonies and the housing areas, they generally get some food. I asked the same farmer, "In which place animals don't get food? And where do I find diseased animals. I need to pick them and get them here. I have already talked to a doctor.

He excitedly said, "In industrial areas, sahib."

I thought for a minute and said, "You are right, because that is the only place where animals get to eat plastics and chemicals, which causes harmful diseases."

He asked me to take his truck to collect those animals and a few people from the village also were there to get them to the place.

I began this unusual and complex dream from the same puppy, for which Aashi had argued with Aadi. After searching for around one hour, I found the same puppy near the house.

People were watching me, but it didn't matter to me anymore. I didn't care about what they thought, or what they said.

After doing a lot of hard work, I collected animals from several areas of Agra. I preferred those animals which needed medical assistance more. I had contacted the doctor near my house and asked to come for routine check-up. The total was around six dogs including that puppy, three cows and one pig. Most of them needed proper care regarding good food and good medical facility. When I was arranging all these things, I felt a bit crazy but in the evening when the farmer served proper feed to all of them, I saw they were eating greedily. I was happy now. But that reminded me of Aashi; that she will not be there to see this forever, I felt guilty and depressed.

After finishing the work, I told that same farmer to spend the night in my house and take care of those animals.

I didn't take a bath and it was 9:00 p.m. when I reached the hospital. The entire family including Aliya was sitting in front of Aashi, she was feeling better. They all were having conversations with Aashi.

I entered the room and Aashi shouted, "Where were you stupid? I was missing you."

I smiled and said, "I had some work."

"Come and sit with me, I need to talk to you. I don't have much time," Aashi said.

After hearing these words, a graveyard silence fell on the room.

Aashi held my hand and said, "Neev it's obvious that within 2-3 days I will be no more, so I want you to marry someone as soon as possible." I know that you don't know how to wash clothes, how to iron them, and you always remain dirty. So have a break and move on in your life as soon as possible."

I was continuously smiling. And when she finished her talk, I said, "You talk so much even when so unwell. I think god forgot to make the silence button in you."

All the people sitting there started laughing and Aashi was showing her angered eyes.

"Okay okay, keep quiet I want to announce one thing," I said and Aashi excitedly put finger on her lips and said, "Go ahead".

I have some surprise for Aashi at my home; I want her to come there tomorrow in the morning, and I want all of you to come and join. They all started asking what was so special that I was asking Aashi to leave the hospital and move out.

But I didn't discuss anything. Aashi pulled me towards her and said in my ears, "I am your love, baby; at least tell me what it is."

I told slowly, "Sorry love, I can't. It's something special".

Suddenly the same ward boy entered and asked all of us to move. I told Aashi that I would take her outside for half an hour in the morning.

I was waiting for the morning. The second day was over and I had not eaten a single morsel of food. Tonight Aadi would stay in the hospital with me. It was around 1:00 a.m. and I was watching Aashi's face through the glass. It felt worst when we were standing in front of a person who would not be with us. It was like sticking a hot iron rod in the body. I was praying to god to please leave her and take me from this world.

The night was almost over and Aadi was sleeping in the chair. I talked to the doctor about taking Aashi out for half an hour. The doctor agreed and told me to come soon.

I told Aadi and asked him to call all family members at my home. He did as I said. I woke Aashi up and asked her to move. She needed a wheel chair as she did not have that much energy to walk. I took her to the parking on the wheel chair and from there I made her sit in the car.

Within the next fifteen minutes, we reached my house and I saw aunty, uncle, Nisha and Aliya already waiting outside since the door was closed.

I rushed towards the door and knocked. Again I helped Aashi to move out of the car. She was unable to stand comfortably, so I picked her in my lap.

The first thing she said, "Congrats, you have bought a new house, and you have never discussed this earlier."

I said, "Just wait and watch."

The noises of opening the door could be easily heard from outside, all were waiting to see my surprise. Aashi was dying to see. And the door opened.

After seeing all of us, the dogs and cows started barking and mooing, respectively. All the people were shocked, started mumbling, "What is this, Neev?"

I didn't notice and was busy in seeing Aashi's reaction. And suddenly the same puppy ran towards me. Aashi saw all that and started crying. She had tears in her eyes and mumbled slowly, "You are mad, but I love you. I don't know what I should say to you. Please, Neev, don't love me this much, otherwise I will not go."

"That is what I want baby," I kissed her on her forehead.

Aadi came near me and said, "At last you fulfilled Aashi's dream".

Aadi had read about it in my diary, and told the others also.

I was standing with Aashi in my arms and all of the people came near me. They all were saying you really did a great job. The time I was thanking everyone, I realized Aashi was not saying anything. I was busy talking to Aadi and the rest of them were looking at the animals.

Suddenly I moved my eye towards Aashi and I saw she had closed her eyes and tears were falling down on the ground.

I shouted, "Aashi don't cry, this is your dream which I fulfilled for you. I don't know why you are crying."

She didn't respond to me. Aadi too saw her crying. After a few seconds, I realized Aashi was not moving. I mumbled slowly, "Aashi, what happened?"

Still she didn't react to me. Aadi bent down, checked her wrist. There was no pulse. The time he took to say something, his tears started falling down.

I shouted loudly, "What happened, Aadi?"

He started crying and mumbled slowly, "She is no more, Neev."

After hearing those words from Aadi, the environment suddenly changed. Everyone left everything and they started crying.

I was unable to react. Only one thing was going on in my mind: it's not possible. Aadi picked Aashi from my arms as I was in unconscious state. He put Aashi in the car and made me sit in the car forcibly.

My brain was not working properly. I was shocked.

Aadi took us to his home and the rest of the family members followed us in their vehicle.

I was sitting in the corner of the house and Aashi was sleeping in the middle of the hall. People had covered her from all the sides. I was unable to see her. I was not reacting. I was shattered completely.

I was looking at her window, from where she used to show me messages on paper. I was remembering the kitchen from where she sometimes stood up and saw me.

I was remembering the talk of *aloo gobhi*, the taking of blanket for me, spending time with me daily, the style of loving me like a crazy girl. A complete picture was moving in my mind. The tour of Goa, drinking and eating together were all fresh in my mind. I was still sitting in the hall. I had only one thought: It is not possible. Aashi can't leave me alone.

Suddenly I saw some of the people taking Aashi out. I was like abnormal; I rushed towards her and shouted loudly, "Leave her, she is sleeping. If she wakes up then I will kill you all. Don't disturb her."

None of the person heard me; Aashi's mom held my hand and said, "*Beta,* she is gone. And she will never come back now."

I heard her mom and then I realized, "I have lost her forever". I shouted madly like a crazy guy, "Come back, Aashi; don't leave me alone! I can't live without you. I was running on the way the people were taking Aashi. I was running fast and I fell down on the ground due to a stone on my way. I could see Aashi going. I couldn't stand and I was crying loudly for her . I remained on the same place for several hours, but Aashi didn't come back.

It was shocking; I felt my little world had been ruined. There seemed no motive in my life for which I should live. There was only Aashi in my world. She too had left me in this world. If I had something, it was only memories of her, which made me realize she is around me. I could feel her inside me. "My dear Aashi, my love, I will remember you forever. Till my last breath," I spoke as if she could hear me.

Aie waqt apne gam mein, Na shareeq kar mujhko,
Ki tanha huaa hoon , ab chal sakungnaa nahi

September 2011

"Hey Sam, why are you so quiet?"

"Nothing, Neev. I am sorry for your loss."

"Stop it, don't cry. You promised me to give some suggestion and you are crying."

"Neev, you are so different. It will be difficult to find a guy like you these days. How can you love some girl that much?"

"Sam, there is love in every heart. The people are the same with the same heart. Just tell me, for what should I live in this world without Aashi?"

"I know it's very difficult for you to live without her; but do you want to end all her love with ending your life? If anyhow Aashi gets to know about your suicide attempt, will she like your desperation? She would never want you to do this."

"So what should I do, Sam? At every moment, I die a thousand times for her. How do I live so long a life?"

"Just manage yourself, live for those animals that are dependent on you for food and medical treatment. Will Aashi ever want you to leave those animals free again as they were earlier? Just start your life again and have confidence. Try to spread love among people and one day you will find someone with the same soul of Aashi's."

"Yeah, you are right dear. Well, I hope I could follow your words."

"Neev, please don't say hope; you have to live. You know god has allotted some good time and bad time for everyone. And you know for sure that your bad time is over. Something good has definitely been decided for you and you will see it sooner than you can imagine."